Sea-Change on the Solent

by Jim Figgis

Dorrance Publishing Co
585 Alpha Drive
Suite 103
Pittsburgh, PA 15238
Visit our website at *www.dorrancebookstore.com*

ISBN: 978-1-4809-1225-0
eISBN 978-1-4809-1547-3

SYNOPSIS OF BOOK
SEA-CHANGE ON THE SOLENT:

The book is a novel about a family in which the father finds himself unemployed and the family has to move one hundred and fifty miles to find work.

Chapters 1-3:
The first three chapters introduce us to the family, starting with John, the father, and his search for work, after months of unemployment. One day he is surprised to be invited to attend a job interview, and in a short time the family decides that he should accept the job being offered and move to the south coast of England, where the job is situated.

The remaining chapters of the book deal with the following:

The move and all it involves, with John, the father, taking temporary residence to be near the work.

Millie, his wife, gives notice to terminate her job as a school secretary and puts their house on the market.

The parents, with Rachel, aged 12, and Edmund, aged 9, visit the town where they will be living, called Lymington, in Hampshire.

They make an offer for a house, and their old house is quickly purchased. John, meanwhile, has started his job as a sailing instructor.

The family takes temporary residence, and Rachel and Edmund explore the town with their mother.

Millie looks at and chooses two schools for her children. Before the start of the term they have to look again for a school, and choose a school run by a Christian Trust.

Edmund is invited to an evening youth club for boys run by a member of the staff, and he also begins to attend their church. He invites his parents and Rachel to go with him to the church.

Rachel takes up riding on Sundays while the others go to church.

Barny, an old school friend of Edmund's from his last school, writes to him and invites him to visit him over the school holidays. Barny tells him that he has been praying for Edmund and his family.

Edmund's housemaster asks Edmund to give a three-minute talk to the school at assembly.

Rachel has taken up learning the violin, and practices at home.

Edmund one day tells his mother that he has "found" the Lord. She is skeptical.

Rachel is advised by her music teacher to give up riding, and concentrate on the violin.

In the end, both the children do well, and Rachel wins a music scholarship to study the violin.

Edmund, meanwhile, leaves school and decides to go to the university of his choice, with a view one day of becoming a missionary.

Their parents look back on the years spent bringing them up with grateful thanks.

BOOK TITLE: "Sea-Change on the Solent."
STARTED 11.2.13 by Jim Figgis

A novel for older children and grown-ups. Topics include pony riding, sailing, and some deeper things of life.

THIS IS A STORY about a family of a mother, a father, and two children—Rachel, aged 12, and Edmund, aged 9—who are living somewhere in the Midlands of England. It also includes a young friend of Edmund, who appears in the story from time to time, and who has an influence on the way things eventually turn out for the family.

AUTHOR'S NOTE: The name "Rehoboth," which comes from the book of Genesis in the Bible, means "space," or "The Lord has made room for us." The school of that name which plays a part in this story is entirely fictitious, and has no connection whatever with any other school which has that name, and any likeness of any kind to such a school is unintended.

Contents

Part 1

Chapter 1

John Perfect has an opportunity

John Perfect was sitting one day near the window of his house with the newspaper spread out in front of him. He was not working that day, and in fact had not worked for several weeks, after being made redundant at the car body shop where he had worked since passing out as a qualified paint sprayer some years ago. Several times he had responded to job advertisements in the paper and elsewhere. Every time the answer came back that they didn't require any paint sprayers at that time.

The job centre near where he lived had leaflets which gave details about training courses in the area for people who wanted to train for new skills. If he went on one, he thought, what was the chance of a job at the end of it? Would he go through all that, work for a few weeks, and then be made redundant again? This had happened to people that he knew, and the outlook for jobs seemed just as bleak as ever that morning as he sat there, wondering how they would live comfortably again once his savings ran out.

Then the phone went. "Hello, is that John Perfect?"

"Yes," he replied, hoping it wasn't an unwanted caller.

"Would you be interested in teaching people to sail dinghies? Your CV says you have an interest in sailing and an Inshore Sailing

Certificate. There's a possibility that you might be the person we're looking for."

"I'm interested in any sort of work for which I might be considered qualified," said John.

"Can you come and meet me at a hotel?" said the voice. "We can meet there and talk about the job, and you can consider whether you want to apply for it."

John took details about the interview, and said he would come. The hotel was thirty miles away, and he would have to find his own transport. His car was off the road, so the journey would have to be made by bus.

John collected together certificates and other details and photographs of his sailing experience, and when the day came, he was waiting at the bus stop very early, in case of transport difficulties.

Arriving at the hotel about two hours later, but still in good time, he ordered a cup of coffee at reception and sat waiting for his interviewer to turn up.

A voice called out, "Are you John Perfect?" The speaker had just entered through the main hotel entrance. "I thought we could go downstairs where it's a bit more private. Bring your coffee with you, and we'll go down together."

The interviewer, a man about his own age, forty or thereabouts, introduced himself, and they sat down in a lounge area which adjoined the hotel conference suite.

"I work for an employment agency, and we specialize in unusual job openings. We were sent your details, and I'm glad you were able to come this distance to meet me."

John looked interested, and took out his CV and other papers from his attaché case to show the man. At this moment he wasn't sure how far he wanted to go in showing interest, but tried to show enthusiasm.

"The job is based at Lymington, on the south coast," the man said, whose name was Clive. "Of course, you would have to move house, to be near your work."

John did not react, but thought of his wife and children, and the upheaval of moving, changing schools, and having to make new friends.

"There aren't many people with your interest and qualifications who are also looking for work of this nature," Clive said. "The last holder of this job was a lady who left rather suddenly. The person who was her employer is naturally looking for someone who can start right away."

John said he would have to give it some thought and consult with his wife and children to see how they would feel about moving a hundred and fifty miles to the south coast. Then another thought entered his head: he might lose the opportunity if he showed hesitation.

"The employer will be able to meet you here tomorrow, if you wish to apply for the job," said Clive.

John saw the job beginning to slip away if he didn't reply in the affirmative.

"OK," he said. "I'll be here this time tomorrow. Would the same time suit?"

Clive dialed a number on his mobile, and was put on hold. A few seconds later, he was put through to the employer.

"Hello, Charles. I have a suitable man for you who wants to meet you here tomorrow at around this time. Would twelve o'-clock suit you?"

The appointment was agreed, and the meeting ended.

So, John was walking on air as he left the hotel and immediately phoned his wife, who was at home for her lunch.

John knew in his heart that if the job was to be his, his wife and children would have to agree to it, with the inconvenience of having to move a hundred and fifty miles and change the children's schools. He also knew that by being positive at his first interview, and not hesitating, he was probably more than halfway to getting it.

Chapter 2.

The Family Discussion

John Perfect's wife was at home when he arrived back at about 4:00 p.m. The children were out playing with the children next door.

Millie, his wife, worked as a school secretary, and shared most of John's interests, including sailing and travel. Some of their neighbours and friends had also been out of work in the recent recession, which was sending some businesses into oblivion. She and John were happy that they still had her earnings to pay for their main expenses.

John was jubilant, and fully expecting to be offered the new job as a sailing instructor with a reputable South-Coast sailing school. There remained the full interview next day with the employer, reference checks, and Millie's agreement to the change of lifestyle and relocation. She would also need to hand in her notice at the school where she worked, and hoped that this would not cause a delay to their going. Moving house to a more expensive area would be a jump that she and John would just have to take, believing that a desirable three-bedroom house would come on the market just as they were needing one. If not, they could rent, if it were possible, and they would be under financial difficulty anyway until their own house could find a buyer, as it still had twelve years of the mortgage to pay.

"I know you want to have this job, John," she said, as they sat to discuss the matter. "And of course, if this house didn't sell, we could rent it out, which is sometimes the only option."

Before telling anything to the children, they thought that John should accept the job if offered, provided that the salary was enough, and there was time to enable her to hand in her notice on leaving her job, and hopefully to find a buyer or a tenant for their house.

In walked Edmund, their son, aged nine, hungry and thirsty, his tongue hanging out like a dog that had just run ten miles. Rachel, his sister, twelve, followed, in more orderly fashion. Meals were usually a family affair in this household, so Millie told them to get a drink or something to keep them going until a meal could be gotten ready. Meanwhile, John was peeling vegetables, cookery being one of his other specialties. Millie forgot at once not to tell the children.

"Your Dad may be going to get a job on the South Coast," Millie told them, "and we will have to move house. Of course, we'll have to find new schools for you as well," she added. "The truth is," she went on, "there are no jobs for paint sprayers here anymore."

Both of the children tried to speak at once, so Millie restored order, and let them speak one at a time, the oldest first. She first told them that it was not a done-deal yet, and that they must wait and see the outcome of the second interview tomorrow.

This news calmed the children down, and instead of coming up with lots of questions, they both ran into the back garden to play with tennis rackets and a ball.

Rachel spoke first. "I wonder what the schools are like on the South Coast. Will they be mixed, or all girls?" she asked. "It's near the New Forest, so perhaps we'll be able to get a pony."

"Are ponies free?" asked her brother. "Can you just find one and train it and keep it?"

His sister thought that was most unlikely. "You don't get anything for nothing," she replied.

After the meal was over, with little more being said about the proposed move, John and Millie looked at the internet to see what the housing market was like in the area of Lymington. Their fears were correct. Prices were mostly quite out of reach, unless they could find some way of raising the extra money.

"It will depend on what we can both earn," John said. "Unless something out of the blue turns up."

The Second Interview

Up early at the bus stop the next morning, John thought of the other jobs he had applied for without success. "I hope this is the one for me," he thought. He arrived at the hotel just as a large motorbike came round the corner, stopped, and a bearded man got off. John walked up to him and spoke first, and introduced himself. To his relief, the rider of the motorcycle was indeed Charles, the owner of the sailing school at Lymington.

Clive was waiting for them inside the hotel, so they all sat down in the lounge where they had sat the day before. Clive ordered coffee.

"I see you two have already introduced yourselves," Clive said. "How were the roads?"

Charles was enthusiastic. "Like a dream; just the outing I needed, instead of sitting in my office all day."

"How about you, John?" Charles asked, turning to him.

"Quite good," he said, "but going by bus is not my favourite means of travel. At least somebody else has to think about the other traffic."

"It can be horrendous during the morning rush hour," they all agreed.

"What sort of job are you looking for?" Charles started with. This was a test question, because only one job was on offer.

"I understand you have a vacancy for a dinghy sailing instructor," replied John Perfect.

"And you think you might be the person to fill that vacancy?" Charles asked. "Do you have teaching experience?"

John said he was used to teaching first aid to the scouts. He had already gotten a police clearance in order to do this, which is a requirement of Health and Safety regulations. This job would involve teaching both children and adults.

"Good," said Charles," because that might have held up your application if we offered you the job."

They discussed John's sailing experiences, and what his ambitions were. Then they moved on to discussing the family, and the ages of his children.

"How quickly could you sell your house and move down to the Coast?" asked Charles. Now it was getting warm and John was definitely encouraged.

"I think we could get on with that right away," said John.

"How is the mortgage? I suppose you have one?" asked Charles.

Now things are definitely moving to a conclusion, thought John.

"When can I start?" John asked after answering the previous question. He was now putting his prospective employer on the back foot.

Not wanting to be pushed, Charles replied, "I'll let you know by Saturday by telephone. First I must consult my partners. I'll definitely phone you at about ten or eleven on Saturday morning.

As the interview closed, both Clive and Charles thanked John very much for coming to meet them, and Clive said, "You won't have long to wait before you hear."

Chapter 3.

The Wait for An Answer.

John arrived back home and started to mow the grass. The family was nowhere to be seen. His children had gone to adventure training, it being Thursday, and today they were going to learn about hill-walking in winter conditions. Millie, his wife, had stopped off after school at her mother's, which would take her about half an hour. There was not much to say to them when the evening came, and the children seemed to have forgotten all about the possible move.

Friday passed, and then came Saturday morning, and the expected telephone call. Millie went shopping, taking the children with her, to keep them occupied and out of their father's way.

As if by an automatic machine, the phone went, and it was Clive, as he expected. "How are you," asked Clive.

"I'm fine, thanks." Pause.

"Well done, they have offered you the job, so can I take it that you will accept it?" asked Clive.

"When do they want me to start?"

"As soon as you can get yourself down there. The salary is as mentioned already. What do your wife and family think about it?"

"We both feel that it will be a good move. I forgot to ask if there is a pension scheme, and whether the company gives any assistance for moving house and buying a house."

"I'll have to come back to you on these things. Does this mean you are still undecided?" asked Clive.

"No," replied John, "I accept the job as discussed yesterday. We are both very happy about the proposed move, so it would be up to them, whether they could help us out with the move as a helpful gesture, and if there is no pension at the moment, perhaps they might be persuaded to start one in the future. We see it as an act of faith, properties being higher in the south, but are willing to take the plunge, and see what happens."

There was an atmosphere of elation, mixed with wonder, when all of the family was reunited on returning home. The children went straight on the internet to find out the names of schools and all the other things they could discover about the town they were soon going to live in. John rang a South Coast house agent, asking for details of suitable houses within a short distance of his work. Millie then spoke by telephone to her mother to give her the news, and then her two sisters, both living not far away.

It was probably the first time in his life that Edmund had not finished his plate of soup and asked for a second helping. He could not wait to break the news first to his friends next door.

New Forest Wildlife. Butterflies like these are common there
1. Pearl-bordered Fritillary
2. Common blues
Found in clearings on sunny days in summer
(Photos by Owen Figgis)

Chapter 4.

House-Hunting

To the reader: You have seen how the job-shortage had affected the Perfect family in their home in the English Midlands. Especially this is the case for a skilled worker who has a family, and hopes to maintain the same standard of living for them. Then there is the long wait, sometimes never-ending, for a job to come up. But, here is a man with flexible ideas, and many skills which he had not considered before, and a wife and family who are backing him up, although she will lose her job as a school secretary. The children are at an important time in their lives, but are quite content to consider losing their school and friends out of wanting to see their father happily back at work and earning. After all, the family's future was at stake, and its ability to provide for its members through adulthood and old age.

• • •

The next thing was to phone a local estate agent where they lived and put their house up for sale. If any further help was needed to tell people, this action would certainly tell the whole town that the Perfects were about to move, because the advertisement would appear in their local paper.

John went and saw the owner of the garage who was repairing the car. "Ready by Friday," was the reply. The garage owner had heard that they were moving, and added, "If you want to, you can trade this car in for a bigger model, and I won't charge you anything. I know someone who is looking for a smaller car like yours. This might help you in your move, with your growing family."

Next day was Sunday. The conversation in the Perfect house was all about moving. The children spent a long time sorting out their belongings, deciding what to keep, and what they could leave behind. They decided they would go and see the car which had been offered in exchange, and quickly made up their minds to accept it. On Monday, John calmly drove it home.

Particulars of houses for sale in Lymington on Sea started to drop through the letter-box, which added to the sense of anticipation in both parents and children. "We must go and see what they are like," they agreed, but still mindful of the need to sell their own house first. Taking a borrowed tent and some basic camping gear, they drove off for the South Coast late on Friday, ready to begin house hunting.

The children were both tired and rather sleepy when they drove home on Sunday. There was less excitement, and a slight sense of boredom about, when they could see that they could only possibly choose one out of several houses they had seen. "Best to wait, now," said Millie, "rather than act in too much of a hurry."

So, the days followed, with offers of one house after another, and then the day arrived when a buyer appeared with an offer for their own house. It was a family like their own, who needed to live near the new quarry which had opened a mile away. This was the much-needed step that they wanted to help them on their way. Would negotiations take long? Would their banks hurry the process?

Chapter 5.

John Goes to Work and Gets Some Help

Meanwhile, John's new employers wanted him to start work. Accordingly, he said goodbye to his family one morning and started for the coast. He arranged to stay in a hotel until a house could be found. Now that the house move had started in earnest, he thought again of approaching his boss, Charles, about getting help from him financially over the move.

"We were thinking about helping you if you still needed it," Charles said. "We will certainly pay for your hotel visit, and would suggest you take lodgings instead, if buying a house does not happen straight away." John thankfully agreed, and began his first day's work, which was a tour of the boatyard, and introductions to the other instructors and boat-maintenance men. He made himself familiar with the different types of fiberglass dinghies, some of which were new to him. Next he was shown the chart room, and the main dangers along the shore as shown on the chart. Then Charles took him out in the motor rescue launch to see for himself where the navigational dangers lay and where the tide-races were.

During the rest of the first week he began to teach sailing to school groups, mostly numbering no more than five, and using the larger dinghies to accommodate that number. The Sailing

School was open on Saturdays for private clients who were learning to sail, and also in the school holidays. There was also a cruising section, in which owners of cruising yachts could organise off-shore cruising and obtain tuition at the same time. John could see that the family interest in nautical things was soon going to receive a boost, when he could get the ideal house they all wanted.

Chapter 6.

John's Wife Meets His Landlady

Millie and the children drove down on the weekend to be with John, and began to look for lodgings for him. It didn't take long. The landlady told Millie that she would love to take all of them, if it would help, while they still didn't have a house. Next, Millie contacted the heads of two schools which they had heard about, and they both gave them a tour of their school premises.

The main thing now was to complete the sale of their own house, signing and exchanging contracts through solicitors, and contacting a removal firm, who would be able to store their furniture prior to their finding the house they wanted to live in. For the next few weekends Millie came down with the children, who were beginning to feel more as if Lymington was their home. She only had to work at her job until the end of term, which was fairly soon, and then she and the children would be free to get their belongings packed and ready for the removals firm so that they could move out.

John, meanwhile, was getting accustomed to working on the boats, and getting to know the tides and currents which come and go in the Solent, the stretch of water which separates the mainland from the Isle of Wight. Anyone new to sailing a boat there can be surprised by the effect of the tides and currents in the area, especially when you sail a small sailboat.

Millie and John were constantly telephoning each other during this time, being aware that the move was fast approaching, but also that the business of moving house didn't seem as stressful as it's often supposed to be. Every few days, what could have been a huge burden to Millie or to John turned out instead to go quite smoothly. A furniture dealer turned up one day, after hearing that they were about to move, and offered quite a lot of money for the pieces of furniture that they had decided to leave behind. A friend of the family offered to buy some of the children's toys and cast-off clothes. The replacement car which they had bought in exchange for the old was a marvel of engineering, and easy to drive. Best of all, Millie's mother seemed totally relaxed about their moving, and her two sisters likewise, who would be available to assist their mother in case of emergencies.

Chapter 7.

Moving Day

The summer term was nearly over, and Rachel and Edmund counted the days to go until the holidays should start and the move to Lymington. The other family was coming to move in to their house the following day. They all had very mixed feelings about leaving the place and the friends they had known for most of their lives. John was away teaching sailing all week, and this meant more responsibility for Millie, being still at her job as school secretary, and having to write or email everyone about their coming change of address. The number of people needing to be informed of this seemed endless. She also filled in a change of address form at the Post Office, for redirection of their mail.

Her colleagues at the school where she worked, and also some of the parents, joined together to make a presentation of some money to help them with the removal costs and solicitor's fees for the sale of their house. On the day itself, John was able to have a day off, so that they were able finally to leave and arrive as a family in Lymington. Some of the children's friends came to the house to give them a tearful farewell (especially the girls) as they left.

Finally, they had heard of a house to buy which filled their requirements, and they had an appointment with the house agent that same evening to look at it. Arriving in Lymington, they first left their luggage that they had brought with them with John's landlady, who had agreed to give them rooms, and went straight to find the house agent.

The house he showed them was in a quiet street, and had a smaller garden than their last house, but seemed just what they were looking for. It didn't take long for them all to agree that they should take it.

"A letter came for you, which I forgot to give you," said their landlady to John when they returned to the guesthouse. John looked at his wife as he stood there opening it, and out came a cheque for a large sum of money, made out to them both, and a note from the sender, in which was written, "For you both as you move house, in recognition of our friendship over several years."

The family took this kind gesture as a sign to them that they should not hesitate, but proceed at once with the purchase of the house they had seen. In fact, it was only halfway through the school holidays when the agent's formalities had all been completed, and they were able to take possession of the house and move in with their furniture which had been in storage.

Chapter 8.

The New Place

"I knew," said Millie, as they all sat at breakfast in the guesthouse dining room the next day, "that this move would be the right thing for us to do. Everything to do with the move has just fallen into place, and we have hardly had to worry about anything."

"I like it," said Edmund, "and the cat that lives here is extremely friendly, and came up to my bedroom this morning to see me when I was getting up."

"I want to go and see the house again, the one we are going to buy," said Rachel.

"Well," said John, "I'll be off to work now, and see you all again this evening." He could hardly suppress and contain his excitement as he saw his family all in such good spirits, having no regrets, and the prospect of their finally owning a house again not far off.

While John was out at work, Millie and the children decided how they were going to spend their time in their new surroundings, with only the guesthouse for their base for some time.

After less than a five minutes' walk, they were looking at the shops in the town centre and taking a note of the different buildings there, which included the swimming pool, gym, and library. Wandering on, they saw some street names which sounded quite historic and with a nautical flavour, such as Captain's Row and Nelson Place. They tried to imagine what the town had been like in the days when sailing ships called there, and the press-gangs came round the streets, bribing men or forcing them to join the ships as crew, for the long voyages from which many sailors never returned, having been shipwrecked or taken captive and made to serve as galley slaves in the ships of Turkey and Algeria, when they still had oared galleys, and to fight in their wars.

They sat down at a table in a café for refreshments and noticed that the house had once been a public-house called "The Saracen's Head". Another house across the road was called "The Bosun's Locker," where all sorts of curious and exotic things were on display for sale.

"I think this is better than the market at home," said Rachel, forgetting that Lymington was now her home.

On their walk they went in the library and saw some notices advertising local holiday activities for children. Rachel and Edmund studied them carefully, hoping they would be free for them to join.

Their mother said, "Actually, Dad said that you can join a week's sailing course at the Sailing School at half price, and we will pay for you, if that's something you would like to do."

The children looked at each other, before Rachel spoke.

"I would like that very much. It's all so easy to get to, and does not require buses and things."

Edmund agreed. "We might even get across to the Isle of Wight."

It was only a short walk to the Sailing School from the town-centre, and there they asked to speak to Charles, the owner.

"Good morning," said Charles, "I understand you are here to book your children into a week's course, and that they have done some sailing with you and John before."

Charles would not take any deposit, but said if the two would like to start tomorrow, wearing suitable clothes, plus a spare set, they would be most welcome.

That evening at the guest house, their landlady was taking an interest in the children's plans to have sailing lessons and invited them all to have some tea with her in her own sitting room, where the house cat made a straight line for Edmund and spent the next hour sitting and being stroked on his lap.

Chapter 9.

The Two Children Begin a Sailing Course

Arriving early the next day with their bags containing spare clothes, Rachel and Edmund sat down in the reception area of the Sailing School, ready to begin their first sailing lesson. Already there were some other children and adults getting their life jackets out of the store and were busy putting them on.

A man they had not met before greeted them and told them where to leave their spare clothes and led them into the adjoining classroom, where other children were already sitting down. A moment later a young woman came in, dressed for sailing, and introduced herself to the children.

"Hello," she said, introducing herself as Helen. "Most of you are starting the course today, and a few of you started yesterday. There will be three boats going out, and I shall be with some of you who are starting today. My colleagues, Tom and Mike, will be in charge of the other boats. Those of you who were here yesterday, please stand up and go with Tom to your boat, while the rest stay here for a few moments, while I run over some basic safety procedures with you."

When the others had left, Helen spoke again.

"Welcome to your first sailing lesson at this school. We hope you will learn a lot about sailing very quickly, and enjoy yourselves at the same time. We have a big reputation here for turning out excellent sailors, and I may warn you that apart from being quite hard work to learn all that we shall try and teach you, you may find yourselves getting very wet and uncomfortable, not to mention seasick occasionally. Firstly, you must learn to put on your life jackets correctly."

Helen soon found that the children were following what she was saying, and began, with the aid of a chart, to teach them some basic terms for the parts of a dinghy, so that they could understand the instructions she and Mike would be giving them when they were out on the water. It was all common sense, really, and Rachel and Edmund quickly saw the importance of learning to do things her way.

They also learned what to do if they fell overboard, if that should happen, which was most unlikely, and not to catch their fingers against the jetty when the boat was arriving or leaving.

"Did you see how those other children who came yesterday seemed so quiet and well-mannered?" Edmund asked his sister, as they followed Helen and the rest of their small class.

About half an hour later, the three boats were out on a wide stretch of water, about one kilometre downriver from the Sailing School.

"We left just before high tide," said Helen, "and I want to get us back safely before the ebb tide picks up, and gives us trouble getting back. In an emergency, I would request the rescue boat to come and tow us back, but I hope that won't be necessary today."

The tide being high and slack, she gave each person a turn on the tiller, to see what it felt like to steer the boat. The wind, which had at first been very light, then started to strengthen, giving the boat a heeling motion, and a considerable increase of speed, as they tacked, or zigzagged, across the mouth of the river. Spray flew over the bow, once or twice landing on the children, who were not worried about a little water, but enjoying it immensely.

When the time came to return they had the wind on their backs, and the boat rolled along with its canvas sails spread wide. Helen warned about not standing up when the sail passed over their heads, with its heavy boom.

She tested their memories on the things she had taught them. "Why do things have funny names on boats?" asked Edmund.

"No reason," she said, "they just call them those names and they sort of stick."

The two other boats were following a little way behind. Then some lighter dinghies came along behind them and overtook them.

"I can see Dad steering one of those," said Edmund. Their father was in charge of a group of five very fast boats, built for racing. As they watched, the leading boat turned round a floating marker buoy, and headed out again to sea, followed closely by the other four.

"When you have had a lot more experience," said Helen, "you will be ready to try one of those, but not until. When they pick up speed, they can be very difficult to stop."

It was time to return to the Sailing School, and Helen showed them how to stop the boat by bringing it round head-to-wind, and lowering the sails at the appropriate moment, just before reaching the jetty to come alongside. She timed it so that the on-shore wind pushed the boat towards the jetty, without the help of the sails. The two other beginners' boats came up behind and performed the same maneuver.

Millie was there waiting for them at the Sailing School. Edmund noticed once again the difference between the two other groups of children. One group was pushing and arguing, while the other group walked calmly back to the store to return their life jackets. Tom, their instructor, obviously knew the group he was in charge of, and as they all left, they got into a minibus with the name of their school painted on it. It was REHOBOTH CHRISTIAN SCHOOL, with its phone number painted on underneath.

Chapter 10.

The Third Day at Lymington

The children were asked to sit down again in the classroom on the second day of the sailing course to brief them on some more safety items before they went out on the water again.

"Did you notice how we get the sails up and down?" asked Helen, the sailing instructor. The children did not know the answer, or were not prepared to say if they did.

"First, you untie the rope we call the halyard," Helen said, pointing to the chart of a dinghy. "The sail won't come down until you do. If the wind was to increase suddenly, I would ask one of you to lower the sail, so that I could put in a reef. That is the term we use for rolling up some of the sail to make it have a smaller area. What effect do you think that would make to the boat?" she asked them.

"It would slow it down," one of them answered correctly.

Then she showed them one of the batons, pointing again at the chart.

"These batons are for stiffening the sail when it is in use, so when we reef, we must take out one or more batons if necessary. To reef the sail, we wind it around the boom by hand."

Helen went on, "You must also stop the boat while you are doing this. We call this 'heaving-to.' This is done by slackening off the main sail with its long mainsheet, the rope we control it with, and pulling on the jib sheet, to bring it close to the mast. That way the boat will slow down and stop.

"If ever we had to stop to pick up a person who has fallen overboard," she went on, "you would need to know what to do. You would have to sail the boat round in a circle, and stop right where the person is. Then you would heave-to, being careful not to run the person over in the water, and throw them a rope, or reach down and help them climb back aboard. We have to be prepared for accidents like this to happen."

The second day proceeded much like the first, with some sun and a light wind from the south. They all took longer turns at the tiller, while Helen taught them the basic points of sailing, i.e. running before the wind, reaching, and beating to windward, and tacking. She also taught them how to stop the boat and heave-to, using the technique they had learned about earlier in the classroom. Then they reefed the mainsail and unreefed it.

On the return to base, each child was given a turn at bringing the boat up to the jetty, gently, without ramming it.

"You have done well," Helen said to them as they returned their life jackets. "Sometimes it takes twice the time to teach what you have learned to do in two days. Tomorrow we'll leave slightly earlier and have a longer trip, and perhaps go out into the Solent for a spell, before we return."

Chapter 11.

A New Turn of Events

Millie and John were pleased that the two children were getting on well with their sailing lessons. The sea air and exercise was doing them good, and they were usually quite tired when it came to bedtime at the guesthouse.

Their landlady brought them a copy of the local evening paper. On the front page there were reports of two fires that had been started, it was thought by vandals, at two of the local schools in Lymington. One was the Primary where Edmund was due to go to in the new term, and the other fire was at Rachel's High School. As a result, no new pupils would be taken at either school, due to the damage caused by the fires and the pressure this would put on classrooms.

"This means that we will have to think again," said John, as Millie and the children took in what had happened. "We shall have to look at other schools," they all said at once.

Next day, while John and the children were at the Sailing School, Millie got on the telephone to some of the other schools in the area. She was able to find that all of them answered her calls, even though it was holiday-time. She also got details about independent schools in the area and the special points about each of the schools. She had not yet given much thought to getting herself a job, but knew that she would have to soon.

The guesthouse was now full of holidaymakers and their families. This was a source of much interest to the Perfect family, as they saw new arrivals turning up with their suit-cases and being shown to their rooms. Some came with very little luggage, while others came with a lot, including sports equipment, binoculars, even telescopes and bicycles of all description. Every evening the dining room was full, and the staff was running in and out serving meals. Most of the guests appeared again very promptly at breakfast, and regaled their appetites for the day ahead, with more and more slices of toast and cups of coffee, to follow the standard cooked breakfast. Rachel and Edmund were amazed at how much some of them were eating, and wondered whether they all ate like that every day when they were at home. As for themselves, they did themselves pretty well also.

Chapter 12.

Possible Schools for Rachel and Edmund

Millie had made appointments to see two of the schools on the same day. Both were within about ten minutes' walk. The heads of each school were going to show her some of the children's work, as well as all of the facilities for music, recreation, catering, etc. When she had seen them, she was tired, and went to find a cool café in the town, where she could rest and refresh herself.

"There seems to be a big difference," she told John that evening, "between the general atmosphere and objectives of the two schools. The high school has very good aims, and achieves well, judging by the prizes and trophies which are awarded each year on a house system, and quite a large proportion get into good universities. But I could not help getting the feeling that the pressure put on the children to achieve high marks in academic subjects has a spin-off effect into the morale and well-being of the underachieving minority. I think that this may account for the levels of crime and vandalism which we've seen already. It must be hard to run a school, but I would like to think that all the children were being treated equally, and not some at the expense of others.

"The Christian independent school, on the other hand, seems to have set its sights on making every child an achieving child, who will benefit from his schooling long after he has left school. Those who are bright and quick to learn generally get where they want to go in the opinion of the head, while the rest find there is something for them to suit their academic level. Both schools have craft workshops for various crafts, as well as music and art rooms.

"We discussed the fee system, and it doesn't sound as insurmountable as I thought. Both Rachel and Edmund stand a chance, having had a good school record up to now, of getting a bursary award, and this makes a considerable difference. The head told me that the exam for these can be arranged at any time, if we should be interested."

John looked at his wife and thought for a moment before speaking.

"If you are thinking what I'm thinking," he said, "we ought to arrange a second visit, with the children, to the Christian school, as soon as their sailing week is finished. From what I know about school bursaries, they need not be very difficult to obtain. Mainly, you have to answer every question you have been asked to answer, and not any more. Keep a cool head, and look over what you have written, in case of silly mistakes, and write neatly."

The children were then asked if they liked the idea of the Christian school, some of whose pupils they had already met at the sailing school. One attraction was that the ages at the school ranged from 8 upwards, so they would both be there together, making the journey to school easier.

This was quickly agreed, and so it was that on the following Monday, at 2pm, the two children turned up for their bursary examinations at Rehoboth Christian School, which was situated about five or six minutes' walk up the hill at the back of Lymington. John and Millie, both being quite keen on their children's success, had spent some of the weekend giving them some simple spelling tests and math tables tests, just to sharpen up their mental skills in case they might have slipped back in these skills since the start of the holidays.

Part 2

Resume of PART 1. The story began with John Perfect, an unemployed paint sprayer from a Midlands car factory in England, looking for work of any description. A chance phone call from a stranger who ran an employment agency led to his being offered and accepting a job on the South Coast as a sailing instructor. His wife, Millie, and their two children of school age, agree to the move, which takes place one summer.

Chapter 13.

The New School Year Approaches

John and Millie Perfect, and their two children Rachel and Edmund, twelve and nine, did not mind not having a holiday. Partly this was because, with John being unemployed for several months, holidays had not even been talked about, and partly because the excitement of having moved from the Midlands to the South Coast was providing them with all the holiday they needed, at least as far as the children were concerned.

John was making himself very useful to his new boss Charles at the sailing school, and was kept at full stretch taking classes out sailing from 9 a.m. each day except Sundays, and sometimes during the long warm summer evenings as well. Millie had her work cut out making things for the new home, which they finally moved into before school started for the autumn term. Rachel and Edmund had already made some friends through the sailing school and from going on nature walks with a local group of children which they had seen advertised. It was a beautiful part of the country, with the sea and the New Forest close to each other, and the best possible time of year to be enjoying it.

The bursary exams for Rachel and Edmund's school were now over, and they were waiting for their results. Millie had been several times to the job centre and had had two interviews. One of these was as school secretary in a large girls' school, and she was still making up her mind about what to do. The hours were most attractive, so that she could have holidays coinciding with the children's. Her previous similar job in a Midlands school obviously counted in her favour. The money would be needed to help pay the mortgage, and also school fees for the children. It depended on whether they were awarded bursaries. If not, she would look for something with a little more pay.

Then the letter arrived from the Rehoboth Christian School. It was from the Chairman of the Governors of the school, and it gave them the information they had been hoping for, that the Board of Governors had seen the children's exam papers, and had decided that, in their cases, the normal fees for pupils would not apply, on two grounds.

First, both Rachel and Edmund had submitted neat, well-written answers, showing clear thinking for their ages, and without a single spelling mistake, and their arithmetic had been faultless. Second, the Board had decided to increase the normal award in view of the special circumstance of their family having to relocate 150 miles to find work.

In view of these considerations, the Board had decided to make them both bursary awards amounting to the whole of their fees, their only expense being for school lunches if these were required, and the cost of any school trips not being part of the general curriculum.

Millie and John breathed a huge sigh of relief when they read this news.

"It's one more thing that has just gone in our favour," said Millie.

"It's really excellent news," said John, "and I think our two have thoroughly deserved a free place, in what seems to be an excellent choice of school."

The children were beside themselves with happiness, which can hardly be described. Rachel ran to her Mum and burst into uncontrollable tears, her feelings were so emotional. As for Edmund, he ran upstairs to his bedroom, closing the door behind him, and spent the next half-hour writing a letter to his best friend at his last school that he had left behind, 150 miles away.

And Millie phoned the Girls' High School to say she was still interested in the job of school secretary, if it was still on offer, to which she received a positive answer at once.

Chapter 14.

First Day at the New School

With only six days left of the school summer-holidays, and the cooler weather typical of August in England, business at the guesthouse was starting to slacken, and one waitress now covered four tables, where previously there would have been seven tables every evening, with two serving. So the landlady was delighted to hear from John and Millie when they phoned up and asked if they could book a table for four one evening, before the start of the new term. This was, of course, a way of celebrating the way everything had recently turned out: their new house; John and Millie both finding jobs; and their children being accepted into their school on very favourable terms. In fact, to welcome them back, she put four small candles on their table and lit them, which was something that had never been done before in her memory. It was the first time since coming to Lymington that the family had eaten out in the evening, and it turned out to be an evening that they would remember. It also happened to be Rachel's birthday, she being now thirteen, and the cook had not been slow in producing a beautiful birthday cake in honour of the occasion. All the other guests joined in the birthday celebration, and each person was given a small piece of the cake and wished Rachel many happy returns of the day.

Rachel and Edmund were now looking forward to going to their new school, but not without certain feelings of apprehension. The Headmaster said they could come in any day before the start of term just to get a little more familiar with the place and its extensive grounds. Millie went with them, because she was as keen as they were to find out what the school offered in its many departments and facilities.

Then the day itself arrived, when Rachel and Edmund arrived with their school bags bearing a few essentials, and were met by a crowd of children of all ages, as they assembled in the main hall. Millie was not with them because she had her own job to start in her school, which was also within walking distance.

"What were your first impressions, Rachel?" asked Millie when they were together at home after school. (Would she be silent, like some teenagers become when asked a question they're not sure how to answer, thought Millie).

"The teachers were all nice, and I made some friends," replied Rachel, "and the morning assembly began with prayers and hymns, and then quite a long talk from the Head."

Then she turned to Edmund, who was on his third sandwich, and asked him the same question.

"I like it," he replied" "but the assembly was a bit long."

"Perhaps you will get used to it," Millie said, "when you have made a few more friends. By the way, a letter came for you today."

Edmund swallowed the rest of his cup of tea, took the letter and thanked her, and departed upstairs to open and read his letter.

"Dear Edmund," the letter began. "Thanks for your letter. The holidays are nearly over here, and we are all keyed up about school. I will be in a new class, and there are going be to be lots of new kids. I am taking up the violin. I have been playing golf during the holidays. I see you have been sailing; that sounds good fun. Let me know how you like your new school. We were praying for you the other day. Yours ever, Barny."

"Mum," he said when he came downstairs again, "some of the boys go to an after-school club on Fridays at 6 p.m., and I was asked if I would like to join."

Millie asked him if he knew who ran it, and where it took place.

"It's at the drop-in centre in the town, and it's run by Mr. Long," Edmund replied.

Millie then said he must ask his father, but she would not mind him going. She had met Mr. Long, one of the teachers at the Christian School.

John Perfect came home just after that, and Edmund was ready with his question.

"Hi Edmund," he said, "let me sit down first, and hear all about your first day at school. Did you learn anything today?"

"Oh, yes," Edmund replied, "and the assembly went on a bit, with lots of prayers and a long talk from the head. I am starting French and Latin, and there is a good swimming-pool."

"So you quite enjoyed it," said John. "And what is happening on Friday?"

Edmund told him all he knew, which was not very much, except that half of the boys in his class were going to it.

"That's good," said John, "I like that idea. You will get back here as soon as it's over, I trust."

It was Rachel's turn next, and she told him about the different teachers she had met, and the other children, and the subjects she was doing.

She showed him the homework she had been given, and had already started, and mentioned that she was going to begin taking violin lessons.

As the week continued, Rachel and Edmund were finding out what they needed to learn to catch up with the other members of their classes. At first there seemed to be a lot of things they could do as extras, such as a nature club and a recorder-playing club, both at lunch-times. It seemed too much to do at first, so they both decided to wait and see what their friends were doing, and not to start doing too many things at once.

A violin
(Photo by Jim Figgis)

Chapter 15.

Edmund Goes to Boys' Club

Friday afternoon came, and at ten-to-six Edmund found three newly-made friends standing at the gate waiting for him to join them on their way to the after-school club.

They found there were some other new members like Edmund, who were not from their school. The drop-in centre was run by the church, which the other boys all went to with their families on Sundays.

"This is the night for nine- to twelve-year-olds," explained one of them to Edmund. "Come inside and meet the other boys."

There was already a group preparing for a game of basketball, and others sitting at tables playing chess and doing jigsaw puzzles. After about half an hour, Mr. Long, who was in charge, called all the boys over to have refreshments at two long tables. While this was happening, and they had said a prayer of thanks together, his helper, who was also his wife, read a chapter from the Bible, which was from one of the Gospels. Then followed a time of questions, to see what the boys had understood from the Bible-reading. Mr. Long then picked up his guitar and started to play and sing one of the songs they had learned at school. Following this, the boys were organised to do some team games, and this lasted until it was nearly time to finish. Before they left,

Mr. Long got them all sitting down again, and said a few short prayers, for the town, for their schools, for their families, and for anyone in difficulty or sick.

Edmund was asked whether he had enjoyed his first visit to the club, and he gave an enthusiastic reply. In a few minutes they were back outside his house, and he said good-bye to the three boys who had come with him.

"Are you coming to our church on Sunday?" asked one of the boys, as he was making for the front door of the house.

"I'll think about it," called back Edmund, and he went in and slammed the door behind him.

Chapter 16.

Shopping Trip

Millie and Rachel were going to do some shopping on that Saturday, and asked Edmund if he would like to go with them. There was quite a large covered market which had all sorts of stalls where they sold a great variety of things on Saturdays. The children were very interested in the pets stall, where there were things like hamsters and snakes in cages and glass containers. Millie was ready with what to say if the children asked her to buy one.

"You must save up for it first," she said, "and then you must promise to buy its food and look after it properly." They both thought about this for a moment. Rachel needed new trainers, so went to try some on. Edmund was looking at a pile of books and comics nearby. Just then they heard some music starting up, and recognised two of the girls from their school who were singing some rousing songs in an open space near the market, accompanied by their parents, who were playing violins, and some other children from their school.

Millie asked Rachel if she knew any of them, and Rachel said she would like to go and listen to them. Soon they were all three joining in with the singing, the words of which were displayed on a large flip-chart poster for all to see. At the close of the singing, the father of the girls stood up and gave a talk. Instead of using a microphone, he just used his voice, which was quite a strong one. After that, they sang some more songs, the crowd of onlookers growing all the time.

Then, from a nearby street appeared a group of young men and women who seemed determined to give trouble by starting a rival singing group nearby. As the singing from both groups became louder and louder, and the crowds thicker and thicker, it became obvious that the group from the children's school was attracting more attention than the other group, which, after a few minutes, broke up and disappeared in the direction from which it had come.

"They seemed as if they were trying to break up the other group," said Millie. She wondered whether this sort of thing went on often.

That afternoon she and the children spent at home, and Edmund tried out the lawn mower, which his father had been showing him how to work. Later, when they were all together, John Perfect asked everyone for ideas of what they would like to do tomorrow, the first Sunday of the new school term, and his and Millie's day off.

"We could take a picnic to the sea-side," suggested Millie.

"We could see if there are any ponies for hire," said Rachel.

"My friends from school go to a church on Sunday mornings, and asked if I would like to go," said Edmund.

"Why don't we try all three?" said John. "We could all go to the church first, then see if there any ponies, and take a picnic with us and eat it wherever we find ourselves."

That evening Edmund wrote again to Barny, back in the Midlands. The letter went,

> Dear Barny,
>
> Saturday

Thank you for your letter. I thought about using email to write to you, but this is much more private. The new school is cool. I have made a few friends, and I went to their club on Friday evening. Tomorrow, we are all going to see them at their church in the town. This morning some children were singing songs in the market place, and some other people tried to drown them out by singing something else at the same time, but it didn't work so they left. I hope you are having a good term.

Edmund.

CHAPTER 17.

WHY GO TO CHURCH?

John had once been a churchgoer in his youth, but had stopped going when he was about eighteen, as so many young men do. He had been a choirboy and then a bell ringer. He only felt a little bit guilty about his lack of attendance. Instead he felt quite virtuous about having attended church all his youth, and he could do without it quite well now.

Millie was from a similar childhood, and had been keen on Girl Guides as well. However, as she grew up, she saw easily through some of the actions and attitudes of her leaders, to whom church-going was no more than a ritual which they followed week by week, mainly for appearances. Like John, she worked hard at her job, and was glad to find time at weekends to take up activities which left no time for church on Sundays, and seemed just as beneficial.

They married when they were both in their mid-twenties and became very taken up with making a home, which involved a lot of do-it-yourself and shopping trips to a variety of local shops at weekends, which catered to homemakers. As many of these, including garden centres, were open on Sundays, no time remained for the old system of church attendance, and this was the experience of most of their friends. With car ownership also, life had many more exciting possibilities than sitting for an hour on a hard church pew and participating in a service which she had heard many times before.

It had started to awaken Millie's conscience, when at about this time after they had just moved house, she became aware that there was a new generation of churchgoers, who did not have a problem with the older, more formal, and stuffier generation of worshippers, because most of these had either disappeared due to age and infirmity, or death, or had thinned out to the extent that they were barely noticeable any more. With careful scrutiny, she noticed that some of the upcoming church groups among her neighbours were now showing a more tangible and genuine character, which was more to be expected from a people known to be churchgoers, with always some exceptions. However, she still maintained at this time that she could live a moral life, giving no one offence, and raising her children in a self-sufficient mould of their own creation, without having to resort to an institution like the church for their nurture and guidance.

It took, in fact, a considerable effort on Millie's part to swallow her self-sufficient pride, and the same also applied to her husband, when they both agreed to go on that Sunday morning with their small son to a place of worship on the first Sunday of the new term. Their daughter, Rachel, not having yet had time to established a routine of teenager self-sufficiency, after so few weeks in her new home, and being only just in her teens, was happy to give anything a try, so long as there was no call at the moment for a permanent commitment from her. She was still young enough to feel a certain hesitancy when it came to making decisions about her life, and was not at that time conscious of losing face if she were to be guided along by the prevailing family mood.

After all, what is our life, but a succession of events and pressures, which we respond to differently according to different impulses at the time, like a rubber squash ball which is propelled at a wall at great speed, only to be sent back on a different trajectory by another, equally powerful force, until it completes its journey and becomes dormant and lifeless, and is placed back in its dark little box once more?

So it must have seemed to Rachel Perfect, as she lay in her bed that night, contemplating the events which had moved her and her family so rapidly, in that eventful summer of her thirteenth year.

Chapter 18.

They All Attend Church

The cats in the surrounding neighbourhood of John and Millie's house in Lymington-on-Sea that Sunday morning seemed more than usually contented and were looking for somewhere nice to sleep after having just had quite a sumptuous feast from more than one overflowing waste-bin, which had received certain quantities of fish bones, heads, and innards on the evening of the local open flounder-tramping competition, held annually on a Saturday when the tide was at its lowest at that time of the month of September. The gulls, for their part, had also had quite a field day, having been joined by certain reinforcements in the shape of cormorants, shags, shearwaters, guillemots, and other, more exotic seabirds, which are sometimes found in those waters, but further off-shore.

Edmund's three friends came calling for him a quarter of an hour before service time at their local church, which was also exactly the time when the four members of the Perfect family were just on the point of setting out for that very same destination. It only took five minutes to get there, so the family and their escort of boys had plenty of time to mingle with the other hopeful worshippers before going inside the building, which was already resonating with the sound of a guitar and drum band, accompanying some very tuneful quiet singing of devotional music. John thought it was quite tasteful, and an improvement on the kind of music, usually played only on the organ, which he had grown up with. Millie felt it was a little over the top. Something a little more traditional was more her taste.

Instead of being shown to a seat in the auditorium immediately, they were offered a cup of tea or coffee, with biscuits, and a choice of cool drinks. This enabled everyone to relax and meet if they wanted to, or they could sit quietly in a reading area nearby. Some of the members of the congregation, acting as ushers, were seeing that everyone was met and greeted, and made to feel comfortable. The children, of various ages, were mostly sitting quietly in groups, or chatting to each other, and enjoying their refreshments.

After a short while, one of the church members came over to John and Millie and invited the family all to come and sit in the main auditorium, as the main service was about to begin. The rows of seats, which were individual chairs rather than benches, soon filled up so that the front half of the auditorium had very few spaces left. At this point, the man who led worship introduced himself and the members of his band and pointed to a large screen above his head, containing the words of the first hymn. The choir, assembled in a crescent behind the band, immediately, at a signal from him, burst into a loud praise song, in which most of the congregation joined. Singing in close harmony, the words, "Praise Him!" were repeated four times, followed by a silence. Then came another line of the song, containing much the same message of exuberant praise. A longer pause followed, and the pastor, who had remained inconspicuous until then, took over, and started to pray, inviting people to enter with him into an expression of quiet reverence, with the intention that people who had concerns or guilt on their minds could find release by bringing their burdens "to the Cross," where the blood of Jesus Christ, God's Son, cleanses us from all sin.

Then followed a few prayers, in which those who had need to repent of their sins would receive complete forgiveness and the promise of a new life in Jesus Christ, who died to save us from our sins. Other prayers of an uplifting nature then followed, encouraging all Christians to love one another, and to remain steadfast in the faith.

More singing and more prayers followed. Then the youth leaders stood up and invited the children who were going out to their Bible classes to go with them. Rachel and Edmund went out with them also.

A sermon began at this point. The pastor welcomed all newcomers, of whom there were several, including the Perfects. His text for his sermon was Isaiah 8:17, "And I will wait upon the Lord, that hideth His face from the house of Jacob, and I will look for Him."

The room was fairly full of eager-faced adults by this time, including some who had come in late, as he proclaimed his message with a loud, clear voice, with only one or two notes on the desk in front of him. To John, this was different from the kind of preaching he was used to hearing back home in his youth. It had clarity, and an urgency, and carried with it a strong conviction, just as if the preacher was speaking the very words of God. John began to imagine he was hearing the voice of a prophet, like John the Baptist, as the pastor began to challenge the congregation with similar words to, "Who has warned you to flee from the wrath to come? Every tree that fails to produce good fruit is hewn down, and cast into the fire."

Everywhere there appeared on people's faces looks which said, "What shall we do?" And the answer, coming straight from Matthew's gospel, loud and clear, was, "Repent, all of you, for the kingdom of heaven is at hand. Show in your lives good fruits, pleasing to God, after you have thoroughly repented, and start to live new lives afresh in Christ. New wine must be put in new bottles; the old ones will not do, they certainly will not, because they will burst."

The sermon continued in the same vein as he illustrated it with examples of people he had met in his work and gave examples from his own life before he knew Jesus Christ as his Lord and Saviour.

Returning from time to time to his opening text from Isaiah, he asked the people, "Are you waiting upon the Lord? Is He hiding His face from you? Are you really looking for Him? Is He answering you? Do you expect He will answer?"

If ever there was a moment in that morning service when there was hardly a dry eye in the church, this was it. Silence followed the preacher's voice. When he spoke again, it was to invite anyone who needed to see him privately for a few moments afterwards, could do so in the vestry adjoining, or by telling one of the ushers that a private meeting was needed.

"My phone number is on the printed sheet," he said. "We run a telephone enquiry service for all those who want to discuss things over the phone, and it's free."

There was then another hymn to close the meeting, during which the tithes and offerings were collected by the ushers.

Later, at home, the two Perfect children were able to tell Millie and Rachel what they had learned in their Bible classes, who they had met, and the names of their teachers. Both seemed quite keen to go again.

"I'll see what my friend Liz is doing next week," said Rachel.

Chapter 19.

The Perfect Family Settles Down

Dear Barny,

Thanks for your letter which I just got.

We are now on the third day of our second week at our new school. My teacher is quite strict, and likes us to write neatly. She teaches us French, English, and math. I also have a Latin teacher and a science teacher. Every day begins with an assembly led by the head or his wife. We sing plenty of songs I did not know before. I had to see the head the other day, and he asked me if I went to church and read my Bible. He gave me some Bible-reading notes to get me started.

We also do sport every day before going home at 5 p.m. I am practising long-jump. There is hockey and volleyball. We also play football, but there are no matches against other schools. We have a PE teacher who is cool, and the other teachers help him. The girls mostly do their own sports.

We all went to church on Sunday, and it was really nice. We broke up into little groups, and heard a Bible story. Mine was doing Noah and the flood, which our teacher said was a very important story to learn. He is going to test us on it next week.

See you later,
Edmund

• • •

The work at the Sailing School where John Perfect worked continued into the autumn term, and one or two new staff members had joined since John came. Other staff members were now taking their holidays of two weeks, as demand for instruction had decreased with the end of the summer.

Some people were planning cruises for themselves and their husbands or wives in cruise boats which they partly owned or were going to hire. One couple owned a yacht which they kept moored on the Mediterranean and visited twice a year. Another couple was taking their family next year to sail to the Shetlands to leave their boat there and fly home.

Millie's school was at its busiest as the new term got underway, with about a hundred new girls to settle in, and four new teachers. She herself, being new, had to learn fast, and to cope with banking the school dinner money and seeing the books balanced. She also had to unpack and distribute the new textbooks which were coming in to the various classes, and see to any tradesmen that were needed for repairs to the buildings and the equipment. She also had to ring suppliers for more stationery and books as needed, and chase deliveries.

Rachel had now made a few good friends, and saw them most days at break-times. Some of them had clubs to go to between lessons and after lunch. She did not go with them, but preferred to sit and read by herself. Edmund was starting guitar lessons once a week, with two other boys. They each had about ten minute's tuition, and then played together as a group. On the other days he played football during the break.

The school had a rule not to send text messages during school lessons or breaks. Discipline at the school was strict, but not often enforced. Minor infringements such as lateness were rare. The children were asked to pay particular attention to the way they dressed, although there was no uniform. Shoes should always be clean, and trainers were not encouraged in the classroom. The school ethos was marked by punctuality and orderliness. Coats should be done up if worn.

Rachel was finding the way the school was run was to her liking. She enjoyed the longer school day, and made full use of the school library. Edmund was usually pretty tired by the time he got home, but got a second wind after his meal. Neither of them found the homework hard.

On the following Sunday, they all decided to give the church a second go.

Chapter 20.

Barny and Edmund Write to Each Other

Here the reader might like to pause and wonder for a moment where the story of this family is going, and why they have been described in detail, with all the changes that have happened to them since John Perfect received a phone call, at his old house, back in the first chapter. Why have they been chosen? And is there a continuing thread linking the events that have surrounded their lives, and, almost unnoticed, given them a head start in their new surroundings on the South Coast of England?

• • •

Dear Edmund,

How are you getting on? It's now a few weeks since I heard from you. How is Rachel, your sister getting on? Do you have a good time at your school, with lots of friends? You don't know this, but I was so pleased that you got into that Christian school. Most schools teach all the wrong things in religious education, and it makes me cross. They don't seem to think there could be another version of the Creation from the one they teach, which denies traditional Bible teaching. In fact they deny much that is in the Bible, and that's a serious sin. My prayers were certainly answered when you got accepted at that school. In fact, the whole church I go to was praying for you and your family.

Yours,
Barny

P.S. Please write back soon.

A few days later.

Dear Barny,

I am writing back in reply to your last letter. Yes, I am enjoying school, and so is Rachel also. You should have been here at the last RE lesson, when I asked the teacher about Darwinism. The whole class sat up when I mentioned it. They all believe in a young earth without hesitation. I am still not sure what I believe.

If God made the stars, how did He put them there? How did He also put the hairs on my head? Is abortion cruel? All these subjects came up.

You said you were praying for us. Would you like me to pray for you?

Thanks,
Edmund

Millie was pleasantly surprised at the way her daughter Rachel and son Edmund had both settled into their Christian school. Never before this would she have imagined sending her children to such a school, with its "narrow" teaching, and slightly, in her view, "blinkered" attitudes to life in general. She was grateful that the school gave them both places when the other schools had suffered arson attacks, and being now taken up with the girls' high school where she worked as secretary, she stopped having any misgivings.

Her husband John, for his part, was much respected by the others at his work, for his practical knowledge of boats and coastal navigation and for his hard work and the respectful way he treated the customers. He had also become quite keen on attending the church, where some of the people went who were connected to the Sailing Centre. This included Charles, the owner of the Sailing School, and his wife and family, a boy and a girl, who were always there on Sundays.

In a particular sermon, the pastor preached most eloquently about the observance of the seventh day of the week, which John thought was very appropriate, as most people get nothing out of Sunday, except tiredness and a hangover the next day. The pastor also told his congregation that God had told Moses to tell the people to "observe all the commandments," "that thy days may be prolonged, that it may be well with thee, and that ye may increase mightily," (Deuteronomy 6:3). The idea of having a long life appealed to John very much, and he agreed with the possible connection of long life with obedience to God. When he later told this to Millie, she was uncertain, as she had heard of people in her time who had lived good lives, but awful things had happened to them.

Their daughter Rachel, now aged thirteen, had started spending her pocket money on taking riding lessons on Sundays. These took place at the time the rest of the family was in church, and they usually met afterwards for a picnic in some beauty spot, when the weather was warm enough. John and Millie were not worried about this. They had met the owner of the riding school, who seemed a very pleasant person, who promised that their daughter would be taken good care of.

Edmund had no difficulty in making friends at church, and also continued to go with them to the club on Friday evenings. He got interested in the study of dinosaurs, and began looking them up on the Internet, and borrowing books about them from the library. He mentioned one day to his family that his friend Barny and his family had been praying for them. This led to an interesting exchange of views.

"Does Barny think he can make a difference if he prays?" asked Rachel.

Millie joined in. "It is very nice of him to do that, but I don't think it will make any difference to us. We all have to choose and decide for ourselves what we are going to do."

John was more positive. "For my part, I think Barny is to be thanked for praying. For months I was without a job, and at my wits' end over what to do. Then suddenly, after I got that phone call from a man I'd never heard of, one thing after another seemed to go in our favour. Our move to this house, the sale of our last one, the job for Mum which she is very suited for, and the school for you two, and the friends you've both made, all seemed to be part of a preordained pattern. I should like to think that this pattern was due in part to the prayers of people like Barny praying for us."

The swifts and swallows that had been making themselves seen and heard all during the summer were now lining up on the wires, preparatory for their annual migration back to Africa. For the younger birds that had just left their nests, this was to be a big trial. Similarly, the people who had been so thick on the ground in the holiday season now seemed to be departing in their droves. The owners of the many cafes and gift shops were still putting out their chairs and tables in the morning on fine days, but for fewer and fewer customers. The cats of the neighbourhood who had fed so well on leftovers when there were plenty of tourists, were now to be seen lurking around in the shrubberies for the unwary small bird or four-footed rodent that might have strayed there unwisely without thinking.

PART 3

Resume of Parts 1 & 2.
The family of John and Millie Perfect, and their two children Rachel (13) and Edmund (9), have recently moved to the south coast of England from their home in the Midlands, where John was an out-of-work paint-sprayer. Millie has found a new job as school secretary, which was what she was doing before, while John, who already had some sailing qualifications, has started as a sailing-instructor with an established sailing school at Lymington-on-Sea, on the Solent. The children are at an all-age school, which they are enjoying, and is rather different from the usual run of day schools, being independent, and having a strong Christian ethos. It seemed that the jobs that suited them, at a time when jobs were scarce, were part of a very favourable series of supernatural events that they could not explain.

Chapter 21.

New Thoughts about Religious Education

Edmund arrived at the school one day looking forward to the RE class, and being able to compare the theory of evolution with the time-honoured, but some would say outmoded, Bible account of the creation of the universe, which he was now learning.

(Source: internet)

How could everything have been created just like that, in a few days, as the book of Genesis says it was? Are there not fossils, and carbon dating, and other scientific proofs which explain that it took much longer? And where did light come from?

(Yes, Edmund, there is the crunch, where indeed did light come from? Does the Bible say that God created the heaven and the earth, and there was darkness on the face of the waters? Where was the light, when there was only darkness?)

Then Edmund remembered a verse from the Psalms which was on the Bible Reading Notes which the headmaster had given him: "Thy Word is a lamp unto my feet, and a light unto my paths." Psalm 119:105.

So, he thought, God created the light, by just speaking the Word: "And God said, Let there be light: and there was light," Genesis 1:3.

If God can create light from nothing, He can therefore cause the beginning and the origin of everything else. Now we all have access to God, through the light which shines out of His Word, the Bible. Believe that, and a whole lot of other things become possible. God is still in the business of making things happen, although He finished His creation in six days!

Yes, Edmund, and one of those things is when someone feels their need for light to lighten their darkness, and prays to God with the prayer, "Open Thou mine eyes, that I may behold wondrous things out of Thy law," Psalm 119:18. And God hears and answers, and the person sees, more and more, the wondrous things which God has promised, and is promising, for the future, to His people, through the pages of His Word. And now some scientists are saying that about 27% of the universe is consisting of "dark matter." That means that they have a figure for the other part, that is, 73%. But 73% of what? Can't they just admit that the universe goes on forever, and has no end?

How blessed you are, Edmund, to have had these things revealed to you at such a young age!

Chapter 22.

An Interesting Childhood

Since she was a small girl, Rachel had taken a keen interest in things all around her, and the story that each thing could tell. Close to her old home in the Midlands there was a road, which ran dead straight for miles and miles. People went there with metal detectors to look for Roman coins alongside the road, and were often successful in their searches. She often used to wonder how they travelled in the old days when the fastest thing on earth was the horse. There were inn signs, too, marking ancient hostelries, where you could still drive a car in through the arch, where the horses, which were available for the coaching trade, had their stables, and could be used when coaches called to get a change of horses. That had all gone, and all that was left was lock-up garages and small workshops. And yet, the coaches had left their mark, as shown by the inn sign, of a way of life long gone.

There were railways, too, crisscrossing the Midlands, some now defunct, which you could sometimes follow for miles on foot, and buy a guidebook which showed what to look for when out walking, and which places were notable for their wildlife. This form of transport had put the coaches out of business, a hundred and fifty years ago or more, but now their end had come, in many cases leaving only an occasional rural halt, with its crumbling platform and station-master's house, now a possibility for a rural retreat for someone seeking seclusion far from the pace of urban living. Some lines still carried trains, and a few of them saw the great high-speed express trains bound for Holyhead,* or for industrial towns further north, which travelled so fast that you could hardly hear them coming.

Slightly older were the canals, a treasured destination for those seeking dragonflies and other insects, or for fishing enthusiasts, and towpaths which you could follow for miles, always leading to a lock, with a lock-keeper's cottage, and places where two canals joined, and a turning-basin where the longest barges could turn. Many of the canals were now restored after the neglect into which some of them had fallen, and were now used by owners of all kinds of small craft at weekends.

The older houses, too, had different stories to tell. In former times, some houses were in fact serving double purposes, with large windows upstairs to let in the light for the loom-workers who worked, ate, and slept under the same roof. In the days before there were synthetic fibres, and cotton was expensive, wool was an important commodity in every town and village for the making of clothes for the rich and the poor, and for finer cloth used for shirts and for lace-making, with always the need for socks and stockings and underwear. Villages today still have surviving rows of older dwellings which have outlived the road-widening, and you can still see the posts and iron fittings for tethering horses along the roadsides, and old milestones, giving the traveler his bearings, and the distances from London and Holyhead.*

Rachel had done projects at her last school on transport, and had learned quite a lot of history from visiting all the local museums.

Rachel's mother, Millie, had encouraged her in going to the various places. She had not had so much opportunity when she

*Holyhead in Wales, on Anglesey, one of the short sea-crossings for travelers going by sea to Ireland, being closest to Dublin, Ireland's capital. Much used before the days of air travel, and when the whole of Ireland was in the UK.

was the same age as her daughter was now. There were fewer museums, for a start, and books on these subjects were hard to find. Her own father had fought in the Second World War and had many stories to tell of his travels, which he liked to tell his children and grandchildren. He had been a Petty-Officer in the Navy, and could tell you the names of all the sea battles which he had witnessed, and the brutality of war, when two ships were pitted one against another, and sometimes there was no time to stop and rescue survivors when a ship sank. She also made sure that Rachel was not alone when she went exploring, as it was all too easy for the young to get into dangerous company. Always better safe than sorry was a motto she was always telling both her children.

Chapter 23.

In the New Forest

The New Forest was almost on the Perfects' doorstep. All those who are interested in birds and butterflies come there from miles around. It's also famous for its variety of trees and wildflowers. Over previous generations many of its trees were felled and removed for ship-building and for houses. Consequently, some areas of the forest have a look of desolation and neglect, but this tends to increase the numbers of wildlife, and their great variety, from large mammals like deer, down to the smallest insects, plants, ferns and mosses. It is also famous for its unique breed of ponies, whose owners give them the freedom to roam, and periodically round them all up for health checks and for counting and marking the young that have been born.

The riding school which Rachel used on Sundays was quite near their home, so getting there was not difficult. It drew in a wide cross section of the town, some older and some younger than Rachel. As each week passed, her enthusiasm for riding increased. Edmund, in contrast, could not be persuaded to take up riding. For one thing, it would use up too much of his scarce pocket-money. The other thing was that none of his new friends went riding. He had taken up an interest in astronomy, which was traced back to the discussions he had had at school over the

Creation. In certain clearings in the New Forest there were places you could visit for looking at stars without the usual glare that you get from streetlights in towns. Some of his friends had joined a club for watching the stars, and there was a monthly meeting run by adults who escorted the whole group to and from the forest after dark for this purpose.

Chapter 24.

Adapting to the New Location

As the nights lengthened, and as the days of their first year in Lymington-on-Sea grew shorter with the changing of the seasons, John and Millie and their children, without noticing it, were becoming familiar with the place and its people, and were forming roots in their new, partly alien environment. It seemed a long time to Rachel and Edmund since they had left their old school, back in the Midlands, yet it was only four months ago. Then there was half-term, and fireworks, and then rehearsals for a concert at Christmas, whose coming seemed to be just around the corner.

Millie was not particularly looking forward to Christmas and New Year. Her mother and sisters back at their homes would be going about their lives as usual, and they seemed such a long way away. It would not be the same at Christmas without them reassuringly just a mile or two away. The journey in winter was really too far to be covered there and back in a day. She was also missing several of her friends.

It was the children who were adapting well to Lymington, especially Edmund, as he marched off confidently to school each morning, with his head full of new ideas about the things he had learned recently. He needed no urging to get a move on. Rachel was coping well with her schoolwork and friends, but had to be reminded to tidy her room each day and take her share in the domestic chores. She missed the parties that she used to go to when they were younger, and came home often in a dream, which puzzled her mother, who could not always see it as part of Rachel's growing up, when physically, she was still only a young girl.

John and Millie were now attending the church on a regular basis on Sundays, along with Edmund. Rachel came with them on days when poor weather had cancelled the riding lesson. John liked the informal style of the music, and Millie, although she found some of the hymns too repetitive, persevered, and began to form friendships with some of the congregation. She did not want to be going a different way from John, when Sunday was his only day off work. Conversations at home began to centre more and more on what Edmund was learning, about which he was never silent for long, and lost no opportunity to increase his general knowledge.

Part 4

Chapter 25.

Barny and Edmund write to Each Other Again

Dear Barny,

Many thanks for your last letter. I had my tenth birthday the other day, and I invited a few friends to a tea party. At school we are learning about Creation, which was all new to me, but I see now how important it is to believe what the Bible says, because this is what was written, and was good enough for the church for thousands of years, and nothing has changed, except that some animals have become extinct, and some have increased in size.

I never saw it clearly like this before, and it has affected my whole thinking about the Bible and about God.

I am going to Friday Youth Club at the church, and again on Sundays with my parents. I am with a pretty cool bunch of kids.

See you later,
Edmund

A few days later, he received a letter back.

Dear Edmund,

It was very nice to hear from you and how you are getting on. I had my tenth birthday also the other day. At school the work is getting harder, and we have a new class teacher called Mr. Forge. He is not a forger, I don't think, but more like a blacksmith, hammering away at us as we learn more stuff. We do a lot of English and math, which he says are two really important subjects. I liked what you wrote about Creation. It is, I think, the foundation of all RE teaching, because if you don't believe what the Bible says about it, you will doubt what it says about everything else. For instance, why did Jesus have to die, when God could have found another way of getting our attention? Some churches miss the whole point about redemption, and how it stems from the sacrifices in the Old Testament. If Jesus had not died the cruel death on the cross, like a common criminal in those days, there would have been no sacrifice made for our sins. His death has made it possible for our sins to be taken away, and the way to heaven is open to all who believe and obey God.

It goes back past Abraham, who nearly sacrificed Isaac, (Genesis 22), to Noah and Cain and Abel, who offered sacrifices. The penalty has been paid for us, if we will believe it, because there is no other way we can be good enough to stand before an angry, but righteous and forgiving God. I hope our RE teacher knows this when she decides how to work through all the other religions we have to learn about.

In your Christian school, do you have to learn about pagan religions? In my state school we have to, because the government says we must. Only about 5% of people belong to them.

Keep on writing, and praying.
Barny

A few days later, Edmund wrote back:

Dear Barny,

Thanks for your letter, which got me thinking. It now seems clear that heaven is open, but from looking at the world and its people, only a small number are going there. Only those, that is, who have believed in all that the Bible says, and have asked God to hear them, and to take away their sins, through Jesus Christ's sacrifice for them. This small number of people are going to stand out from the crowd, by their faces reflecting God's glory and forgiveness, and by their lives being lived to please Him. On Sunday I heard the pastor preach (our usual Bible class was cancelled), and his message came from 1Corinthians 2:12-16. It says that there are two sorts of people: the natural man and the spiritual man. To the natural man the gospel is foolishness, so they hold it up to be scoffed at. We saw this happen in the market square, when a second group of people tried to drown out our singing by singing their ribald songs over ours. They stopped singing when they forgot their words, and they were made to look foolish, so they disappeared. They could not understand our Christian message, because it needs a spiritual understanding, which most people do not have. In another place the Bible says, "The god of this world has blinded the eyes of those who do not believe."(2 Corinthians 4:4.) What do you say?

Please reply soon.
Edmund.

As he wished, Edmund got his reply by the next post.

BARNIE PUTS THE PLAIN TRUTH TO HIS FRIEND EDMUND

Dear Edmund,

You are keen to learn, and I am trying to think of the best reply to send you. You are becoming quite a Bible teacher!

Jesus spoke to the Jews in very clear terms in John chapter eight. Some of them were turning to Him (30). They still had doubts, because they thought that being descended from Abraham almost guaranteed them a passport to heaven. But Jesus told them they were still in their sins, and needed to be made free from their sin and guilt (34-36). Jesus went as far as saying that they were of their father the devil (44), and, because of this, they really did not want to know the whole truth (45-47).

When Jesus told Nicodemus, "You must be born again," (John 3.3-7), the man could not grasp this, because of his pride and his belief in his own goodness. It is the same in many churches around the country today. They say they are Christians, but they have no assurance as individuals that their own sins are forgiven. The only sinless person that ever lived was Jesus Himself. Through hearing His word, and believing on Him that sent Him, we have everlasting life, and shall never come into condemnation. (John 5.24). Do you believe that Jesus died to save you from your sins, and have you asked Him that you may be forgiven for all of them, and that you must be born again, receive new life, become spotless like a new-born baby, and after this, spend eternity with Him in heaven? Have you thanked Him enough for saving you, and for taking all your sins away?

If the answer is yes, go on your knees, and ask the Lord Jesus to forgive you, and to accept you into His family, which is His church. Tell your friends and your Mum and Dad and your pastor what you have just done!

We here in the Midlands prayed a lot for you and for your family when your Dad was unemployed, and we are seeing our prayers are being answered in lots of ways. We still pray for you.

Barny

Chapter 26.

The year goes by.

The new year began in Lymington with a new whiff of promise in the air. John and Millie saw Christmas come and go, and the festivities at their workplaces and at the Christian school where Rachel and Edmund went every day, without ever getting a hangover or having a rowdy party to go to. The sort of Christmas John remembered, celebrating with his work-mates after work, and the end of term school parties, all seemed as if they had never happened. The church, and the children's Christian school, had a completely different way of marking the festive season, one which took the focus away from the things of the world, and on to the things of Him Who made us, and sent His Son to live like one of us, and then to die for us. It really seemed, as the Bible says, like new life from the dead. If only he had known earlier!

With fewer sailing classes going out in the winter weather, Charles, the owner of the school, took the opportunity to run refresher courses on all aspects of sailing and seamanship. These brought in people from a distance, some of whom ran their own sailing schools, or gave sailing instruction in schools up and down the country. The most popular course was in Coastal cruising, bringing awareness to people of the fact that most sailing mishaps take place within two or three miles of the coast. One of the difficulties that people find, who start out to sail, is understanding tidal predictions and learning to follow tidal directions and strengths. Another subject covered in the courses was the weather, and how to be prepared for sudden changes when out at sea. Special classes covered night-sailing and anchoring and the use of different types of flares and the recognition of navigation lights, port lights, lighthouses, and buoys. Special time was also given to chart reading, position-fixing, course plotting, and first-aid. There was even a session given for equipping a boat for a few days at sea, and some tips for making meals appetising even when the weather was putting people off their food. Lastly, a series of lessons on engine maintenance and a course on VHF ship-to-shore radio operating and receiving.

These classes had become an annual event, with some attendees even coming back year after year. Not only were they very instructive, gaining from Charles' long experience, but they were also a means of making lasting friendships in the sailing world. Many of the people who came saw their careers as a lifetime mission. Adding yearly to their stock of nautical knowledge, they were also enjoying fellowship of another kind. Many had had experiences while at sea of a power which they could only explain in divine terms. Small incidents, fire at sea, man overboard, lost at sea, all experiences where a special protection seemed to have been offered them which no earthly reasoning could explain.

One man gave an example when, in a very small dinghy, with two children on board, he entered a busy harbour between high harbour walls against an ebbing tide, with a brisk onshore wind. To gain the right approach, he put the tiller over, gybing as he went, and throwing his weight to the windward side, to steady the boat. From above his head, a voice coming from someone watching his entrance of the harbour cried out, "Well done!" About a half-minute later the coastguard cutter left the harbour at a rate of several knots, and would have run the dinghy down if it had been in the way.

In many such instances, seafarers in boats large and small shared testimonies of deliverances they had received from a source which they all believed in, but most of them found hard to put into words. In the normal way, nobody would advise taking the risks that some of them had taken.

Part 5

Chapter 27.

Their First Anniversary at Lymington

Millie and John scarcely knew how the time went, or where it had gone to, as the day approached which marked the first anniversary of their move to the South Coast. Rachel's fourteenth birthday followed, and Millie could hardly believe how she could be growing so fast. All her clothes and her shoes seemed to belong to someone else. Edmund was hardly recognisable as the same small boy who had arrived a year ago from their old home in the Midlands. He seemed to be growing by the day. Both of them were doing well in their schoolwork, and they were heading into the school library each day before school, checking and putting finishing touches to homework.

They had both been back to their old place in the school holidays for a flying visit, and were able to renew old friendships. When they saw their old house, Millie was momentarily overcome with nostalgia. John, who had not shared this visit with them to their old home area, was in the busiest part of the sailing year. Some of those who had gone cruising over Easter had plenty of stories to tell.

Edmund wrote when he got back:

Dear Barny,

We arrived back home in good time, and all of us enjoyed the trip. I think my Mum was a bit sad to see our old home again, but she has now got over it. It was good to have a chat with you, but the time went past quickly. Are you still enjoying your school? When the summer holidays come, will you be able to come?

Yours,

Edmund. (A short note, time being precious.)

A reply came soon.

Dear Edmund,

It was very good to see you the other day. We are planning a youth gathering at the church here. It will be in the summer holidays. There will be lots of games and adventures to take part in. Some people will be coming with their tents, and will be camping in the church grounds. There will be a portable washroom, one for boys and one for girls. There will be a trek, in which boys will go in pairs to the next town, avoiding the main roads, and walking back again by a different route. It will take most of the day. I hope you will want to come. There will be water polo and horse riding also.

I met a boy who has just come back from a camp which was run by another church near here. At the camp there were several people who came to know the Lord. This is hard to explain, until you have experienced it. Lots of people go all through life, and do not know what I am talking about, and think I am a bit crazy. I think you know what I am talking about, don't you? If you do, please tell me. It may happen to you any day now. Don't let other people stop you from reading your Bible, as it is your best food. When you hear Jesus speaking to you, obey Him.

Barny

Chapter 28.

Edmund's New Experience

Millie was a bit confused when her son Edmund tried to explain that he would like his friend Barny to stay during the summer holidays, and then to go back with him to his family's home in the Midlands to take part in a church camp. Rachel also had her plans, and was hoping to get on a music week with some of the girls from her school. As for John, it seemed that he was loving his work, and seemed so indispensable to his boss Charles, that all thoughts of a family holiday would have to be put on ice for this year.

She was confused again, when the next morning, Edmund told her how he had met the Lord.

"What happened?" she asked.

"I was sitting reading my Bible in my room, and I felt He was near me, telling me to praise Him," he replied. "So I started praising Him, and thanking Him for all the things He has blessed us with, and asking Him to accept me, just as I am, and take away all my sins, just as He did with Paul in the Bible, as it says in Acts 26:18. Not only that, but I felt that Jesus was calling Me to be His special servant, to open other people's eyes, and turn them to Him, from darkness to light, and from the power of Satan unto God."

"That must have been a very special moment for you," said his mother. "Now run, or you'll be late for school. Rachel has left for school already."

Millie was thoughtful for a while, after her son Edmund had left, and sat down to have a second cup of tea.

Chapter 29.

Edmund Is Questioned by His Friends

Edmund was kept so busy that day at school that he hardly spoke to anyone all day, until at last, coming in from lunch break, two of his friends passed him in the passageway.

"Hi, Edmund," one of them said, "you are looking pretty happy. What's up?"

"I've found the Lord," Edmund replied, hardly believing what he himself was saying. "How do you know?" asked his friend.

"I was just reading my Bible, and He seemed to be right there with me!" Edmund replied. "He was so real and welcoming, and forgiving too."

"Who have you told?" they both asked. "Did this really happen?"

"I know it really happened, because I was there when it happened," said Edmund, and he dashed off so as not to be late for his class.

Chapter 30.

Edmund Tells Barny of His Experience

Dear Barry,

I was just reading my Bible, as you told me to do, when, this morning, Jesus was in the room with me, and speaking to me, or so it seemed, because He asked me to praise Him and thank Him for all He has done for us as a family, and for me personally. I found myself asking for His forgiveness for all my past sins, and promising to work for Him. Then, as I was leaving the house, I told my mum, and I also told two boys at school, but so far I have told nobody else. I was filled with a new sense of joy, and wanted to start telling people, so this is why I am writing to tell you as well. It is just like Paul in Acts, when the Lord spoke to him on the road to Damascus, and He told me to tell others, and turn them from darkness to light, from the power of Satan unto God.

Yours joyfully,
Edmund

Barny received this news with great feelings of thankfulness. He had been praying personally for Edmund ever since he first met him four years ago, and his family had all been praying for the Perfect family, at the time when John was looking for work and all during their move to the South Coast. He went and broke the news to his mother, who he knew would want to know about Edmund's coming to the Lord. "Our prayers are being answered," she told him," but we must not give up praying for him, and the rest of his family."

Barny went to his room and prayed before writing back.

> Dear Edmund,
>
> This news is good. As I said in my last letter, you might come to know God any day now, and you have. You have heard from Him, by what you say. Now you must keep reading and re-reading your Bible, because I feel that He will want to say a great deal more to you in the next few days. He will ask you often if you really love Him (see John 21:15, when Jesus spoke to Peter). People may laugh at you, even in your family. People may say you have been seeing things, and advise you to forget it. Have you told your pastor yet? Be enthusiastic when you tell people. Do not be put off by people who say you will "grow out of it." Seek out others who will encourage you. When I first started to tell people that I had come to know the Lord, they did not believe me, but the more people I told, the more real joy I had, as I carried on telling people at suitable moments.
>
> All this is important, but it will not go far without prayer, constant prayer, and memorising God's

word from the Bible, with chapter and verse. I suggest the King James Bible, easily the best, and most reliable. Try and read a set portion at intervals during the day, when you wake up, after a meal, and before going to bed. Choose times when you can be alone.

Finally, be with other true believers for times of prayer together. Join a group that you know and can trust, but be careful of imposters, who claim to be great authorities, but are counterfeit, and do not in fact yet know the Lord. Do not waste time with people like that, because your time is precious, and you have no time to lose.

Barny

Chapter 31.

Edmund Hits Some Difficulties

Some days later, Edmund wrote to Barny again:

Dear Barny,

It has been really hard to find time to write to you. I sit down to write, and then I'm interrupted, and when I start again I'm not concentrating, and I get distracted again. I forget to pray. People are telling me to come down out of the clouds, and my mother has been quite hard on me for not hearing the things she says to me.

My Dad has been understanding, and says that the best way to begin something is to begin. That is what I'm now doing. I have taken your advice to pray and read the Bible. I have read the first chapter of John.

What does it mean, "The darkness comprehended it not," in verse five? Does it mean all of creation, or the people in it? And does "comprehend" mean "receive and understand," as I think it does?

I think we would say "grasp hold of," don't you? Why do people not receive and grasp hold of the gospel? Is it their fault, that they are blind to its truth?

What is original sin? Is everybody guilty of original sin? My Mum says there are good people and bad people, and she tells me if I try, I can be good, and I'll get on well. She tells me I am just the same as before I found Jesus, and she does not believe what I tell her about my experience. Do you think it is because I've had an experience that she hasn't?

I'm trying to believe I am a different person, but it's difficult, when others around me scoff at me.

Edmund.

• • •

That day at school was a difficult one for Edmund. His English teacher told him off for being untidy and not trying. His friends ignored him. He decided he would pray on the lunch break.

"O God, this does not seem to be a very good day so far. I get into trouble, and my friends are taking no notice of me. Please help."

He was in the playground when he prayed this prayer. Just at that moment, around the corner came his housemaster.

"Oh, just the person I wanted, Edmund," said Mr. Rose, his housemaster. "Would you mind sparing a moment, and coming with me into my office?"

They went together into Mr. Rose's office, and sat down opposite one another. Mr. Rose began. "The Headmaster has asked me to find a boy to give a short three-minute testimony or account of something that's happened to them recently, in one of our assemblies next week. I think you are a good person to ask, as you speak clearly. Have you got something you would like to tell people about, and would not mind doing it to the whole school?'

"Yes," replied Edmund, "I have. Can I speak about meeting the Lord?"

"I think so, yes, but I must check with the Head. As it is only for three minutes, I don't think he would want to stop you."

"If I change my mind by tomorrow, can I let you know then?" asked the boy.

"Of course, yes," said the master. "Just see me at about this time tomorrow, and we can confirm the arrangement."

Part 6

Chapter 32.

Edmund's Sister Scoffs at Him

Rachel, Edmund's sister, fourteen, caught up with Edmund as he was setting off for school on the day following, after he had been asked to take part in an assembly at their school.

"Have you been asked to speak to the whole school?" she asked.

Edmund laughed. "Like to swap places?"

"What are you going to talk about?" she asked, ignoring his reply.

"I can't give it away, because that would spoil it," he said.

"It's about your seeing Jesus, isn't it?" she insisted.

"What is bothering you?" he replied.

"Because I don't want to be called the sister of a nutter," was her reply.

Just then, they turned in at the school gates, and were separated in a melee of children going in.

Edmund kept his appointment with Mr. Rose, and said he would speak at assembly next week.

> Dear Barny,
>
> I've got an opportunity to speak about the Lord at school assembly next week. The Bible says that

anyone who is ashamed of Me and My words, of him shall the Son of man be ashamed. Thank you for your letter. It has made a lot of things clearer. Just this morning, my sister Rachel was trying to bully me into telling her what subject I was going to speak on. She seems to think I am off my nut. I am positively looking forward to it, like when Paul was in prison at Philippi, and the whole jailor's family came to know the Lord, including the jailor. Quite an unlikely happening, but I think God likes to do unlikely things. Regarding your advice, I am meeting with other Christians now, including an older man who has taught in a local Bible Class and has run or assisted in Bible Conferences in Africa and in India, and preached in many churches, both here and overseas, and I am reading and learning my Bible. Why is the King James Bible better? I am not afraid of what anyone says, but it is hard when it comes from members of your own family.

Edmund

The reply came in a few days.

Dear Edmund,

You have got a great opportunity to witness at your school assembly, and I pray that nothing happens to stop you doing it. You must know now that you are at the sharp end of witnessing, and Jesus will give you strength to overcome all difficulties. He told His disciples before He left and ascended into heaven, "You shall bear witness." (John 15:27, Acts 1:8). He gave His disciples power and authority over all devils, and to cure diseases, and sent them to preach the kingdom of God, and to heal the sick (Luke 9.1-2). I believe that Jesus has chosen people like you to do just as the Bible says here, as the opportunities come, but the speaking must have first place. "Go thou, and preach the kingdom of God" (Luke 9.60). People won't always welcome it, but they didn't all welcome Jesus, either. He said, in John 7:7, "The world cannot hate you, (if you give in and start to compromise your faith), but Me it hateth, because I testify of it, that the works thereof are evil." For neither did His brethren believe in Him (v5).

Put on the daily armour of God (see Ephesians 6:10-18). This is positively necessary, as too many brave warriors for Christ fall down in the heat of battle, or are prevented from going to fight because of sickness or injury or some other crafty devilish trick. The devil will try and prevent you from doing your assembly. He hates testimonies. "They overcame him by the blood of the Lamb, and by the word of their testimony." Revelation 12:11.

I will answer your question about the KJV, and how it is easily the best, next time I write.

Pray always, don't be alarmed when opposition comes. Greater is He that is in you, than he that is in the world.

Barny

PS Jesus said, "Ye have not chosen Me, but I have chosen you." For all eternity, and "what a man

> sows, that shall he also reap." Galatians 6:7. Praying for you. B.

• • •

On the day before the assembly in which Edmund was scheduled to speak for three minutes, he was just leaving the school gates when a seagull flew by, distracting him. At the same very moment, a motorcyclist shot by, cutting the corner where Edmund was standing, catching the strap of his schoolbag and sending the contents, with the bag, flying across the road.

Picking them up off the ground after the motorcyclist had disappeared round the next bend in the road, Edmund breathed a thank you to the Lord, for guarding him from being hit by the motorcycle.

"Thank you Lord, for sending your angel, to keep me from being hit by that motorcycle." He remembered the words from Ephesians chapter 6 about putting on the armour of God, which he recited every morning by heart, "having done all, to stand." How easily he might have been sent sprawling, or even killed, by collision with the motorcycle, after being distracted by a seagull!

Christ's angel, 1; Hell's angel, 0.

Chapter 33.

Edmund Speaks to the Whole School

The sky was a mass of grey and white clouds scudding along like galleons, as if bent on the invasion of England by some alien army from an unfriendly foe somewhere to the west, on the morning of the assembly at Rehoboth School, Lymington, in which Edmund was due to speak for three minutes. Up earlier than usual, Edmund remembered that several of his friends at his church were already praying for him, that his heart would not fail him.

A piano was playing the opening verse of a favourite Hymn as the school gathered in its usual places, and the master in charge stood up after everyone was settled, and made a short announcement.

"Good morning. We are going to begin by singing one of our favourite hymns, "He who would valiant be," written in the seventeenth Century by John Bunyan. He is famous also as the writer of Pilgrim's Progress, which is now a classic, that is, very widely read, all around the world. After that, I would ask everyone to sit down, and I will ask Edmund Perfect, who is going to speak for a few minutes, to come and stand on the platform, and I want you all to hear what he is going to say to us."

The school sang, and then Edmund was prompted to come on to the platform, and stand next to the master.

Then the master said to him, "Stand here, Edmund, open your mouth, and speak clearly." Without further introduction, Edmund began.

"When my Dad was out of work where we used to live, he applied one day for a job here in Lymington at the Sailing School. When he took the job, he and my Mum and my sister and I all moved down here from the Midlands, and I began coming to this school.

Back home where we used to live I had a school friend named Barny, and we wrote letters to each other. He told me he had begun praying for me. At the same time, my family and I noticed that our move went without any hitches, and both my parents found jobs that were suitable. Also, my sister and I were accepted into this school. Our house which we came from sold very quickly.

"I started to go to the Friday night club, and was told about the church which meets on Sundays. My letters to Barny were going back and forth, as he seemed keen to keep up with me.

"One morning, I was getting up, and reading from my Bible, which Barny had suggested I do, and also some of the masters here. I was getting interested in the RE lessons about Creation at that time, and I was beginning to study what the rest of the Bible said. Suddenly, I knew that Jesus was in the room with me, wanting me to praise Him, and turn from my old sins, and follow Him, showing me also that He wanted me to work for Him.

"I told my parents and I wrote to Barny. Then came this invitation to speak to the whole school about something interesting that had happened to me. Well, this is the most interesting thing, and I know now that I can talk to God any time of day or night, and that He hears my prayers.

"I have now also found out that most older people have never had this experience, and that those who have may expect persecution and ostracism. That is a burden which I must now carry, but Jesus tells us to cast all our cares on Him, and this is what I am now doing.

"Please hear me when I say that I have not been looking for this moment to speak to you all. I was just asked by my housemaster if I would do it. Many things have been happening since we came here, and somehow it is as if angels have been protecting me. Yesterday, I was nearly run down by a motorcyclist as I left the school gates. It was a miracle that he only caught the strap of my schoolbag, and neither of us was hurt.

"I can't really say any more, because all this is so recent, and I trust you will all have the same experiences in time. The school's name, Rehoboth, is from the Bible, and I recommend the Bible to be read and memorised. It may make all the difference in your lives, as it has to mine, and it will give you strength to begin each day with."

There was a mixed reaction from the assembled school as Edmund went back to his seat. Most of the pupils showed no reaction. Some showed scorn in their faces. Some of his classmates showed acceptance towards his message, and some members of staff gave him patronising nods. It was hard to tell who, if any, really believed that he had met with the Lord.

At home that afternoon he told his mother that it went very well. Rachel, his sister, kept out of the conversation. She wanted to hear the radio reports of the latest sporting events. But at the youth club later in the week, he was surrounded by those who wanted to know more. It was the same at his weekly Bible-study group, where the tutor asked him to give a summary of his talk to the assembly to the group.

"Tonight," he said, after Edmund had spoken," I want us to begin looking at times in the Bible where some similar appearances have happened, where certain people have heard direct from the Lord. There are some both in the Old and New Testaments. We shall begin with Genesis chapter two verse sixteen, where the Lord speaks to Adam:

"And the Lord God commanded the man, saying, 'Of every tree of the garden thou mayest freely eat: but of the tree of the knowledge of good and evil, thou shalt not eat of it: for in the day that thou eatest thereof thou shalt surely die.'"

This is the second of the meetings between God and Adam. (The first was when He blessed them, and told them to be fruitful and multiply.) Notice two things. This was a command, which must be obeyed, if blessings are to follow. A dire penalty, death itself, will arise from disobedience. You all know what happened next: Adam disobeyed. Spiritual death immediately followed. He and Eve received the just reward for their disobedience. They chose to disobey God. They could have been obedient, but they, and through them, the whole of the human race, chose the path of disobedience, which disqualified them and us from eternal life and blessings from God in heaven.

Second, God then expelled them from the garden which He had made, the Garden of Eden, in case they should eat of the tree of life (v. 22) and live forever. Their punishment for their disobedience included hard labour for both of them; for her, labour in child-birth, and for him, labour in producing food for himself and his family. There was still a chance to do well, and be accepted again, by faith (Gen.4:7, Hebrews 11:4).

So God has, and still has, the power to destroy or to preserve life. See Matthew 10:28, Romans 2:8-9, and 1 Thessalonians 1:10.

Question: Did they find a place for repentance? (Genesis 4:26c.)

Chapter 34.

Rachel Has a Narrow Escape

It had been very wet in the south of England for several weeks, and the ground everywhere was soft and slippery. One day, when out riding with the riding school, Rachel's pony became stuck in a morass between some trees, and she had to climb to safety by holding on to the branches of a willow tree. The pony was up to its neck, and quite frightened, until at last some firemen were called and they were able to pull the animal out, having first rescued Rachel.

She had no spare clothes, and looked quite a fright when her parents saw her coming out of the riding stables for them to collect her later.

That evening Edmund was reading part of a Psalm which they had read in church that day.

"I waited patiently for the Lord; and he inclined unto me, and heard my cry. He brought me up out of a horrible pit, out of the miry clay, and set my feet upon a rock, and established my goings." Psalm 40.1-2.

Then he continued, "And he hath put a new song in my mouth, even praise unto our God: many shall see it and fear, and shall trust in the Lord" (v. 3).

He knelt down in his room when he went to bed, praying as usual for his parents and for Rachel, that God would bless and protect them, and thanking God for helping Rachel to be safely rescued, and praying that she would also realise where her rescue had come from.

Before he went to bed, he gave a full account in writing in a letter to Barny, of all that his sister had been through that day.

Chapter 35.

Pagan Parades in Modern Britain

Dear Edmund, (from a letter which came to him in reply a few days later)

Your sister had a narrow escape on her horse. Could I have her permission through you to send it to our school magazine? It would look very good when I mention also that you were in church at the time, and that you pray for her regularly. Our news editor is always looking for stories to include in the magazine, and both of you are still remembered here. God has not left Himself without witness, and you are that witness, as were Paul and Barnabas (Acts 14:17). The people of our town today, here in England, are as much into pagan idolatry as were the people of Lystra in the Bible in Paul's day. Why do they have annual parades through the town, with a beauty queen, crowned, and carrying idolatrous symbols, and dressed in a robe embroidered with pagan motifs, while onlookers leer at her from the pub doorways, singing their lewd songs? In 2,000 years the people of the town don't seem to have learned anything better, or to have understood that pagan festivals are the slippery pathway to hell and destruction. Some of our history teachers tell us that ancient Rome was glorious, but they never mention that the rich people kept slaves to do all the hard work, and anyone who rebelled or refused to take part in emperor-worship (such as Christians), were made to fight with lions and wild boars, or with each other (even the women), to the death!

Some of my church will be handing out tracts to people watching the parade, which will explain the eternal perils of forgetting our God who made us and our Saviour who saved us. You must pray for us, that we shall be kept safe, and for good weather on the day. Keep me posted, about your school, and the feedback from your assembly, and about your family.

Barny.

Part 7

Chapter 36.

A Bible Study Meeting

(Up to this point, Edmund and his older sister Rachel, who are attending an independent Christian-run school, have always been fairly good friends. She prefers to go riding on Sundays, while her parents and Edmund go to a local church, although that had not always been their habit. Edmund, aged ten, was invited to speak at a school assembly about his recent experiences, which his sister (thirteen) dismissed as religious extremism.)

At the next meeting for Bible-study, the leader asked if anyone had seen or experienced persecution from religious motives. One family had been living in Sudan, where they had seen violence among local people, where Christians were being persecuted and driven out of their homes.

Following earlier discussions, the reading was from Genesis 26, where Isaac and his family were looking for a place where they could settle, and where they would have freedom to graze their sheep and cattle. The Lord had blessed Isaac (v. 12), and the local Philistines envied him (v. 14). His father, Abraham, had dug wells in that place, but the Philistines filled them all in (v. 15). Isaac then moved on and found other wells which they had also filled in, so he and his servants dug them out again (v. 18). Then they tried digging in the valley, and found a well of springing water.

The rivalry between Isaac and the local tribesmen now grew intense, and again Isaac had to move on. Eventually they found a place where they were not being disturbed and called it "Rehoboth," which means "room." It was here that the Lord appeared to Isaac and said,

"I AM the God of Abraham thy father: fear not, for I AM with thee, and will bless thee, and multiply thy seed for My servant Abraham's sake."

Questions:

1. Compare the news about tension today between Jews and Arabs in Israel with what we have just read about.
2. Is there a prophecy in Genesis which is now being fulfilled?

Chapter 37.

Another Family Discussion

Edmund's mum, Millie, asked him at home later that day what the group had been discussing. The reply she received from Edmund surprised her.

"It was so real, Mum," Edmund replied. "Jews and Palestinians were arguing and fighting over land as long ago as the time of Abraham and Isaac, and their descendants are still fighting over it. It was just like opening the paper, or turning on the news, except they did not have guns then. What helped the Jews was they had God on their side. I believe that is still the case today."

His mother was thoughtful, and did not reply. Then she said, "When Dad comes home, we'll ask him what he thinks."

Then Rachel joined in. "I think they will all blow themselves up, if you ask me," she said.

Just as he said this, John Perfect arrived home from the Sailing School, where he had spent the day like any other weekday, taking groups and teaching sailing.

At dinner they exchanged notes. Rachel was ecstatic because she had enrolled to go on a music week in Devon at half-term in October, and had started saving up her pocket-money to pay for it. This would give her an opportunity to meet some young musicians from several countries and play in chamber music groups with different people. Then Edmund, who found it hard to contain himself up to this, brought up the problems of the homeless people in so many countries, and how people were getting evicted from their homes, and was it sometimes justified?

The discussion went on for some time. John thought there was more than one answer and more than one question here. First, if people don't pay the rent when they are supposed to, then they will get evicted. Second, there could be a legal dispute over who really owns the land and the buildings occupying it. Thirdly, there could be persecution by neighbours driving them out, on grounds of race, religion, or merely local disputes. You even hear of evictions happening under the pressure of someone supporting a different football club from their neighbours.

Millie suggested that some people fall out with their neighbours simply because they didn't happen to have been born in that town or village. Pressure is sometimes put on them to find a home elsewhere, so in desperation they make themselves homeless. Rachel had a friend whose parents had split up, and she didn't now feel like she belonged anywhere. She no longer felt welcomed, because both of her parents had taken on new partners who were not at all friendly to her. Eventually she left home and was taken in by foster parents.

Edmund had been waiting for his turn. "History is full of cases," he said, hoping he did not sound too boring, "where people are driven from their homes by war and famine. Two thousand years ago the Roman armies drove the people of Israel out of that country, and the Jews were scattered into many other countries, wherever they could settle and make a living. They were persecuted severely, so tended to live in communities where they would be safe. All this time, they kept their traditions of keeping special festivals like the Passover, and keeping the Sabbath, which is Saturday."

"Surely, they can't now claim back their land," said Rachel, "just because of having been evicted long ago, before anyone alive today remembers?"

"That's exactly what the politicians are saying, but the Jews can't agree, because God gave them that land, in the time of Abraham, and they have nowhere else to go that they can call their own land. Until the collapse of the Turkish Empire in 1917, it was ruled by Turkey, and was handed to Great Britain as a mandated territory by the League of Nations after the 1914-18 war. Numbers of Jewish people began to immigrate back, until finally the time came for them, in 1948, to declare the new state of Israel."

"So why can't the Jews and Arab Palestinians agree to divide the land?" asked Rachel.

"That would probably be the end of the Jewish state, because other nations in the area of the Middle East want to see all the Jews thrown out of the whole country, and the Jews might find it impossible to resist if they agreed to part with control of any of it. Besides, God promised them all of it, including parts of Syria and Jordan as well, and I believe this promise still stands. In 1967 the six-day war took place, in which Israeli forces vanquished and overcame their neighbours' forces completely in six days."

"Do you really think they won that war because God was on their side?" asked Rachel.

"If you believe in God, you should allow for that, because of all that you can read in the Bible. Besides, Israel also won the war of 1948 and the war of 1973, and since then the Arab nations have learned to respect Israel. Both sides are saying, 'Give the others an inch, and they will take a mile,' so neither side trusts the other, and they learn to hate them instead."

John and Millie were quite surprised to hear their children having such an adult discussion. Millie then asked if they had homework to do, and the conversation ended.

Chapter 38.

Rachel Is Loaned a Violin

The new Director of Music in the Local Education Authority had decided to equip all school music departments under his control with a sufficient number of instruments for all children who wanted to learn, and had even acquired more instruments than the schools needed. These were offered to the independent schools within the area, including Rehoboth Christian School, which had a large music department. As Rachel was needing a violin to take home and practise, she was one of those who was offered one on loan, which she gratefully accepted.

Millie was apprehensive that her daughter's practising the violin at home would upset other members of the family, so she suggested to Rachel that she should only practise for half an hour each afternoon, as soon as possible after she arrived home from school, and Rachel at once agreed.

Edmund posted Barny on what had been happening:

> Dear Barny,
>
> We have been having discussions at school and at home about the problems of people being homeless. Have you thought what it must be like to be

without a home? This is what is happening in war zones like Syria just now. In WWII homelessness affected many people. It is not new. It must be terrible, when we all take our home comforts so much for granted, and then suddenly we have our homes taken from us.

The disputes over land in Israel have gone on for centuries. Have you read about Isaac in Genesis 26 lately? The whole land had been promised to Abraham by God, to him and his descendants, forever. See Gen 15:18, reaffirmed by Moses in Deuteronomy chapter 7. Well, Isaac, the only legitimate son of Abraham, had trouble settling with his family and his livestock, and they were repeatedly driven out by the local people. Eventually they found a place where they would not be disturbed (see Gen 26:22-25). Then there was a famine, and Isaac's descendants went to live in Egypt, where there was plenty, for 400 years, until Moses led them back to Israel, their Promised Land.

In AD70, Roman armies drove the Jews out of Israel, and they were scattered in all directions, including Europe, and many went again to Egypt. For over 1,800 years they kept up their traditions as God's chosen race of people, and in 1948 they regained their land, after long negotiations. For all that time, many Jews were driven out again and again, wherever they went, and were persecuted as unwanted people, so many took the chance that was being offered in Israel and returned there to live and work and build a strong nation again.

Their neighbours in the Middle East resented them and fought to drive them all out, but failed to do so in three brief wars, 1948, 1967, and 1973. As Christians, what now should be our attitude towards helping Israel? They are still in a precarious position, with threats from Iran and other countries. This is a dispute that doesn't seem to have an answer. The leading politicians in the West, UK, France, and USA seem to want a divided state, but neither side is happy with this idea.

The Bible states that God has made a promise, and God does not normally change His mind. These are his chosen people. In Isaiah 41, and many other places, He says, "Fear thou not; for I am with thee: be not dismayed; for I am thy God: I will strengthen thee: yea, I will help thee; yea, I will uphold thee with the right hand of My righteousness....and they that strive with thee shall perish (v. 11)."

We read about the return of Jesus Christ (Acts 1:11) at some date in the future, but people are not often saying where they think this will take place. Bible prophecy suggests that He will return first to the Mount of Olives, outside Jerusalem (Zechariah 14:4), and also to the temple itself (Malachi 3:1). Zechariah also prophesies a siege of Judah and Jerusalem in chapter 12, verse 2. Verse 6 tells who will be the victors in that day. Verse 9 says, "I, (the Lord), will destroy all nations who come against Jerusalem." The rest of chapter 12 signifies a great turning of the Jews to Christ, as they look upon "Me whom they have pierced," i.e. crucified, (v. 10), with great mourning.

I think that the politicians who still support the claims of Palestinians for their own state are going against Scripture, and the Scripture cannot be broken (John 10:35). What do you say?

We may not have a lot of time left, to side one way or the other.

Edmund

Chapter 39.

Rachel Gives up Her Riding

The reply that Barny gave to Edmund's letter in Chapter 38 is not recorded. Current news reports at that time indicated that there was no change in the positions either of the Israeli government or of the Palestinians. The atmosphere around the whole of the Middle East, since the "Arab Spring" when several regimes toppled, remained tense. The support of super-powers was about evenly divided, with Iran seeming to be increasing military support for terrorist groups operating from within Lebanon, and thus creating a serious threat to Israel.

Rachel very much enjoyed her music week, playing her violin and meeting other young musicians from all over the UK, France, and Switzerland. Her musical talents were developing fast, and when she was told by her music teacher that to be a top-rank violinist you must give up all activities, such as horse-riding, which might possibly give rise to injuries to her fingers, hands, and arms. She therefore decided, without hesitation, not to continue riding, and was immediately asked if she would like to join the music group at church on Sunday mornings.

Sundays from then on saw the family all united in church attendance. Rachel did well there, and was soon asked if she would like to lead the music group. As she moved into this position, her confidence improved generally, and the change which took place in her was noticed by all who knew her.

Edmund went to stay with Barny once or twice during school holidays. The town parade was affected by the weather, so that everybody who took part on that day got a soaking. Partly as a result of this, the town May Day Committee decided to call off the town May Day festivities for the following year, and many people heaved a sigh of relief at this development. For years the choice of May Queen had been a source of contention and discord. The Maypole was auctioned off, but received no bids. It was last seen being cut up in a builder's yard in the town.

It would not have surprised anyone to find a few years later that Rachel had won a scholarship to a music college in London and was receiving tuition from leading violin tutors. Nor would it have surprised anyone who knew her to have seen her name included in announcements advertising the lists of the soloists performing in the Promenade Concerts at the Albert Hall.

It is not reported which university Edmund went to when the choice had to be made, but his exam results from his school gave him a wide choice of university places. Eventually it was his ambition to train at a Bible College in the USA, with a view of becoming a missionary with the NASA Space Program.

Their parents, John and Millie, looked back on this period of their lives, when their children were adolescents, with relief and nostalgia. Little did they know, when they left the Midlands for the South Coast of England, how beneficial it would all be.

Barny was happy, too, when he recalled how all the time, since they were young, and when they were all growing up, he had never forgotten to mention the Perfect family in his regular prayers.

THE END

J.FIGGIS, DALBEATTIE, SCOTLAND

Note: The town of Lymington-on-Sea is in Hampshire, England. There is no real similarity in the details of the town given in this book to the real thing. It is not known whether Rehoboth Christian School ever existed.

The Road map of the New Forest was obtained off the internet.

The author takes no responsibility for the political views of the characters in the book.

www.ingramcontent.com/pod-product-compliance
Ingram Content Group UK Ltd.
Pitfield, Milton Keynes, MK11 3LW, UK
UKHW020140250726
13967UKWH00002B/773